HEARTSIDE BAY

THE HEARTSIDE BAY SERIES

HEARTSIDE BAY

Flirting With Danger

CATHY COLE

SCHOLASTIC

Scholastic Children's Books
An imprint of Scholastic Ltd
Euston House, 24 Eversholt Street, London, NW1 1DB, UK
Registered office: Westfield Road, Southam, Warwickshire, CV47 0RA
SCHOLASTIC and associated logos are trademarks and/or
registered trademarks of Scholastic Inc.

First published in the UK by Scholastic Ltd, 2014

Text copyright © Scholastic Ltd, 2014

ISBN 978 1407 14301 9

A CIP catalogue record for this book
is available from the British Library.

Printed by CPI Group (UK) Ltd, Croydon, CR0 4YY
Papers used by Scholastic Children's Books are made
from wood grown in sustainable forests.

1 3 5 7 9 10 8 6 4 2

This is a work of fiction. Names, characters, places, incidents
and dialogues are products of the author's imagination or are used
fictitiously. Any resemblance to actual people, living or dead,
events or locales is entirely coincidental.

www.scholastic.co.uk

Thank you, thank you, thank you
to Lucy Courtenay and Sara Grant

ONE

Polly Nelson's semi-transparent face stared back at her from her aeroplane window. Windows on planes weren't the best mirrors in the world. She looked pale and almost ghostlike. Polly shuddered a bit as the plane bounced. Flying always made her nervous. What if an enormous storm hit and suddenly they were completely at the mercy of the wind?

But beyond her reflection, there was no hint of a storm. The sky was deep and blue and clear. She could see the folds of the landscape far beneath her, reds and golds and greens.

I can't believe I'm nearly in California, she thought.

The last time she'd been in San Francisco, her parents had been in the process of divorcing each other.

It had been painful, and Polly had been angry and sad in equal measure. After the divorce, Polly and her mother had left the States to start a new life in England. Now, more than five years later, Polly's feelings were quite different. Her mum was in a happy relationship with Beth, Polly's teacher. It had been a shock at first, but Polly loved seeing her mum so happy. And Polly had come to consider Heartside Bay home, especially after becoming friends with Lila, Rhi and Eve.

In less than an hour she would be seeing her father for the first time in months. They could catch up properly, spend loads of time together. She would be staying for a whole week on his organic farm north of San Francisco. She'd heard so much about the place, and seen so many pictures, that she had a perfect image of it in her head: the rolling hills, the green valleys, the sweet cows, the outbuildings and the soft Californian sunshine. And Ollie would be with her.

Polly glanced across at her dozing boyfriend. Ollie's head was back against his seat rest, his eyes shut and his mouth slightly open, breathing evenly as he slept. She couldn't resist running her fingers through his thick blond hair, pushing it back from his forehead lightly, trying not to wake him up. He looked so cute when he slept.

Polly had returned to her own natural honey blonde hair colour in honour of their visit. She knew her dad liked the natural colour of her hair. She had been dyeing it for so long – brown one month, red the next – that she'd almost forgotten what her natural hair looked like. If she was totally honest, the blonde felt a bit standard and boring to her. It made her feel a bit invisible, like her plane-window reflection.

"I'd love you even if you dyed your hair blue," Ollie had assured her when she'd suggested going back to her natural colour. He'd complimented her when she'd done the deed and she *thought* he'd been telling the truth, but she wasn't completely sure. Ollie had never made her feel anything other than perfect. Still, she pictured all the California girls they would be seeing on this trip. Girls with perfect white teeth and surfer bodies, long legs and much brighter blonde hair than hers. There's no way she'd feel confident standing next to them.

The other thing making Polly nervous was that this week-long trip would be the first time her dad would meet Ollie. The thought was a little scary.

Dad's guaranteed to like Ollie, Polly reminded herself. *Everyone* liked Ollie. His good nature, his sportiness, his smiling blue eyes. He would fit the whole California scene to perfection. Maybe even better than she did. She smoothed her skirt over her pale knees and wished she'd applied some bronzing lotion to them. Her legs looked like unbarbecued sausages.

As she tried to still the fluttering feeling in her stomach, her fingers went to the locket around her neck, stroking the familiar contours, the silky smooth silver. It soothed her, as it always did. Stroking the locket had become an unconscious habit, and she'd almost worn out the engraved initials on the front. She hadn't taken it off since the moment Ollie had pressed the little box into her hands three months ago, when he asked her out on their very first date. The hinged pendant contained a tiny picture of them both, Polly on one side and Ollie on the other. Even just thinking about it made Polly smile unconsciously. Despite their differences, she and Ollie really did love each other.

But what if her dad didn't like Ollie? She'd never introduced a boyfriend to him before, let alone dragged one halfway across the world. She'd never really had a serious boyfriend to introduce to him before. There had been a few dates with a guy named Sam last year, but that had fizzled out when he had moved down to London. Ollie was her first real boyfriend. The first guy she really loved. She bit her lip and started worrying all over again.

Beside her, Ollie shifted in his seat. Not much worried Ollie. *How does he always stay so calm?* Polly wondered, not for the first time. She felt like she could never make her mind go quiet.

She felt a rush of affection as she studied Ollie's sleeping face again. She'd had a crush on him for so long before they even started dating. She had never believed anything would come of it. They were such different people. No matter how many times he told her that he loved her, she still couldn't quite believe they were together. It was like something from a romantic movie.

Suddenly, the plane gave another jolt, making Polly's heart accelerate in her chest. Outside the window, she could see the wing of the plane moving like the wind was trying to rip it away from the fuselage. All around her, Polly sensed people sitting up, looking at each other, and wondering what was going on.

It's just a bit of turbulence, she thought, doing her best not to give in to the sudden rush of panic that was making it difficult to think. She knew all about turbulence. A family break-up, school dramas, her mother's new partner. She had coped with it all. There was no reason why she couldn't cope with this as well.

Breathing deep and slow helped stave off the panic. Gripping hard on to her seatbelt and shutting her eyes, Polly focused on her breath. In. Out. In.

The plane shook again, more violently this time. Somewhere near the back, a passenger screamed. Polly could feel sweat breaking out on her brow. She was fine. Everything was going to be—

Her stomach disappeared as the plane suddenly dropped like a stone. Outside the window, the ground still seemed so far away – but appearances could be deceptive. Planes were heavy. They moved fast when they fell out of the sky. And when they hit the ground. . .

More people had started screaming now. A baby was crying. Flight attendants had appeared from nowhere, looking anxious as they patrolled the lurching aisles. Polly gripped Ollie's arm in terror.

"Ow," said Ollie, waking up.

"We're crashing," Polly gasped. *Breathe. In. Out.*

"Hey, don't worry," Ollie soothed, rubbing her hand. "It's only a bit of turbulence."

This was not a *bit* of turbulence. This was a *lot* of turbulence. *Things have been going too well,* Polly thought, gripping harder. *My life never stays peaceful for long – I should know that by now.*

"Would passengers please return to their seats and fasten their seatbelts," said the captain through the tannoy.

The world seemed to be narrowing. She felt the material of her seat against her the back of her head. She felt Ollie's fingers in hers. She felt as if her lungs were full of holes. They weren't retaining oxygen, no matter how much she gasped. Ollie was still speaking to her, but she couldn't hear a word. Her vision was filled with little white dots.

She was going to faint. *Maybe it's for the best,* she thought, as the world dimmed around her. She didn't want to know about the moment when they finally ploughed into the ground and burst into flames.

This was it.

TWO

Through the thrumming blood in her head, Polly dimly heard Ollie's voice.

"Keep breathing, Poll. It's OK. You're going to be fine. It's just a little bumpy."

She felt his arms come around her and hold her. The smell of him was so reassuring. The terror of the bumping, groaning plane seemed to recede a little as she let herself be enveloped in his arms. He was there for her.

"There," he said as the bumping slowed and stopped and the plane was once more moving smoothly through the clear blue sky. "All over. We're still in one piece. Turbulence is horrible but it's really nothing to worry about. And right now, I'd quite like to breathe?"

Polly realized her arms were wound tightly around

Ollie's neck. She was almost choking him. The relief of knowing the turbulence was behind them was followed by an acute sense of embarrassment. She let go and smiled weakly as Ollie rubbed his throat.

"Are you OK?" she asked anxiously.

He laughed. "Don't worry about it. I've suffered worse football tackles."

Polly tried to settle back in her seat and enjoy what was left of the flight. She still felt jittery, like an animal in a trap desperate to flee. Except, of course, on a plane, there was nowhere to flee *to*. The awful sense of worry hung about her like a persistent cloud.

It's over. Just another few minutes and we'll be on solid ground, she told herself. But the nervous feeling wouldn't go away.

Ollie touched her shoulder gently. "Look," he said in awe. "I can see the sea."

The sweep of San Francisco Bay curved beneath the plane, the Golden Gate Bridge straddling the water like a tiny, fragile structure of red thread. Polly rested her head on the window and drank in the view. It was so beautiful.

The last time I was here, I was part of a family, she

thought. Images flashed through her mind. Sunlight pooled on a scrubbed kitchen table, the deep blue of the bay just visible from a window in her room, red flowers on window sills, salty Pacific air coming in through open balcony doors. And her parents, shouting and shouting.

"*We should never have come here! I should never have married you!*"

"*If you feel that way, leave!*"

"*Don't think I won't!*"

In her own childish bubble, she had thought they had all been so happy. She had thought her life in this city would last for ever. And then suddenly it was over and the smell of aeroplane fuel was in her nose and her mother was weeping beside her on a plane bound for England. Her family had crashed and burned. An aeroplane disaster all of its own.

Ollie's arm snaked around Polly's waist, pulling her back to the present.

"You're crying," he said, sounding puzzled. "Happy tears, right?"

"Not really," she admitted.

He pulled her head down to rest on his shoulder.

"It'll be different this time," he said, reading her mood. "You're older, and wiser. Your parents are happier apart, you've said it yourself."

That was true, Polly knew. "They were happy together before it all went wrong," she said wistfully. "We had lots of fun when I was younger."

"Fun like what?" Ollie said with interest.

The memories were suddenly coming thick and fast. Polly wiped away her tears. "Dad organized a birthday party with a magician who made birds fly out of his hat," she said. "I was four or five, I think. For months afterwards I would pick up the hats in our hallway and look inside, in case there was a pure white dove sitting in there that I could have as a pet."

"I bet you were cute when you were a kid," Ollie said with a smile.

"I had a very specific ideas about what I wanted to wear, even then," Polly said, reminiscing. "I had this patchwork denim dress with a huge full skirt that I would twirl round and round in so I could see the skirt fly out around me. I would wear it with these rainbow polka-dot leggings. Mum insisted they didn't match but I never listened to her."

"I bet you matched the whole ensemble with bright yellow shoes," Ollie added.

Polly giggled. "You know me too well," she said.

"There's no such thing as too well," Ollie replied, and leaned in to kiss her.

It was still a thrill to feel Ollie's lips on hers. Polly kissed him back happily, then curled up against him, listening to the beat of his heart through the material of his checked shirt.

There was a sudden bump as the plane touched down. Polly jumped. As the plane put on its brakes and began to slow she stared out at the long tarmac runway with its telltale heat shimmer. She hadn't even realized the descent had started, let alone the landing. Ollie had known just how to distract her.

As soon as they pulled into the gate and the captain announced their arrival in San Francisco, people started moving around the cabin, fetching their luggage down from the overhead compartments and gathering together their belongings after the long flight. Polly smiled up at Ollie, intending to thank him for helping to calm her down. To her surprise, he was looking serious.

"What's the matter?" she said, suddenly alert.

Ollie made a face. "Do you think your dad will like me?"

It felt so strange to hear super-confident Ollie asking a question like that. Polly thought she was the only one with hopes and fears for this trip. But of course Ollie would be worried. It was a big deal.

"Oh my gosh, of course he'll like you!" she exclaimed, reaching up to press an encouraging kiss to Ollie's lips. "You're the most likeable person I know!"

He laughed a little ruefully. "Your dad might not see the same qualities in me that you do, Poll. To him, I might seem like the Big Bad Wolf, ready to carry off his daughter."

"Don't be silly," Polly said, giving Ollie a gentle push. "You could never be the Big Bad Wolf. The Little Cute Puppy, maybe."

"Hey! Less of the little, OK?" Ollie protested.

"Fine. The Big Cute Puppy then."

Ollie made a show of thinking about this. "I can live with that," he conceded.

"You make me happy," Polly told him, wanting to

ease his anxiety just as he had eased hers. "My dad will see that, and that's all that will matter to him."

Ollie looked into her eyes. "Do I really make you happy?"

She wrapped her arms around his neck. "You know you do," she told him honestly. "He's going to love you, Ollie. I promise."

Polly bounced on the balls on her feet as they waited in the immigration line. The queue for border control felt like it was taking for ever, even with Ollie distracting her every few seconds with questions about California. She felt a jolt of anticipation as they passed through customs and approached the doors to the main concourse. Ollie was trying his best not to steer the baggage cart into any of the crowd around them. Polly held Ollie with one hand and her rucksack with the other as she pulled him out to the meeting area.

A tall, tanned man was standing at the front of the waiting crowd.

"Dad!" Polly gasped. Abandoning Ollie and the cart, she raced towards her father, who swept her up in his arms and twirled her through the air.

"How's my baby girl?" he said, kissing her soundly on the forehead.

"All the better for seeing you!" Polly squealed, hugging him hard and inhaling the smell of him. She hadn't seen him for months, and now she was here and everything was going to be OK. How could she ever have doubted it?

"I swear you've grown," her dad told her, tucking a strand of her hair tenderly behind her ear. "Now where's this boyfriend of yours?"

Ollie was wheeling the trolley towards them. He lifted an arm and waved a little awkwardly. The trolley promptly swung sideways and almost knocked over a toddler, who was swept wailing into his mother's protective arms.

"I . . . sorry," Ollie stuttered, looking red-faced as he wrestled the trolley to a halt in front of Polly's father. "Not a great start, wiping out a small child. Hello sir, I'm Polly."

Polly's father looked a little startled.

"Dad, he meant to say *Ollie*," Polly put in, giggling. This wasn't like laid-back Ollie at all, to be so nervous and bumbling. It was quite cute, really.

Ollie flushed an even deeper pink. "Sorry, yes. Ollie, I meant to say. I'm not your daughter, am I?"

"I had worked that out for myself," Polly's dad observed.

"It's just . . . we rhyme and. . ." Ollie swallowed. "I think I'm a little jet-lagged," he confessed. "I'm very pleased to meet you sir, whatever my name is."

Polly realized her dad wasn't smiling. She felt a sudden rush of anxiety as she stared at his serious face, and at the way he was looking Ollie up and down.

"It's about time I met the no-good jock who's stolen my daughter's heart," he said.

THREE

Ollie's face drained of all colour, leaving him looking pale and scared. Polly gaped in shock at the angry expression on her father's face. How. . . Her dad had only just met Ollie and already he disliked him?

"Dad," she spluttered, "give Ollie a chance! He's not a no-good jock, he's—"

Her father interrupted with a roar of laughter. "Sorry," he gasped, holding out his hand for Ollie to shake, "I couldn't resist the joke. Your faces, the pair of you! Ollie, son, welcome to San Francisco. I'm very glad to meet the guy who's made my daughter so happy, and I'm sure we're going to have a great time together."

Looking inexpressibly relieved, Ollie shook hands vigorously. "You had me worried, sir," he said as they started heading for the main doors and the sunshine outside. "I was all set to run for the departure gates and head back to England."

Polly breathed a sigh of relief as she followed her dad and Ollie out of the sliding glass doors to the Californian sunshine. She sighed happily at the feel of the sun on her face.

"You've picked a great time to visit," Polly's dad informed them as they packed their bags in the back of a huge brown station wagon parked outside the terminal. "Gorgeous sunshine in the forecast every day this week."

"There's always gorgeous sunshine in California," Polly pointed out.

Her father looked amused all over again. "There's no need to tell Ollie that, Pollydolly. I'm trying to impress him here."

"I thought I would be the one trying to impress you, sir," Ollie supplied, grinning as he held open the passenger door for Polly to climb inside the warm, sticky-vinyl interior of the car.

"Enough with the sir, Ollie," said Polly's dad. "Call me Alex."

Her father's farm was about an hour north of San Francisco, across the Golden Gate Bridge and up through winding roads that wove through the redwoods. As they drove, they occasionally came out of the trees and found themselves alongside cliff edges with breathtaking views of the endless blue water. Polly leaned her head against the window and stared at the landscape unrolling before them: eventually cliffs that shimmered blue in the afternoon heat gave way to rolling fields that reminded her of England on a warm summer's day and vineyards stretched as far as the eye could see. She trawled back through her memory, trying to remember anywhere outside the San Francisco city limits that she might have visited as a kid. Nothing was coming to mind.

Ollie sat beside her, exclaiming for most of the way.

"I love all the small differences, you know? The fire hydrants, the street signs, the number plates on the cars and the size of the trucks. I swear cars are twice the size over here. And the roads! Everything feels so *big*. It makes England feel tiny."

Polly couldn't help but smile as she listened to Ollie's excited chatter. *Everything was going to be fine,* she thought with relief, holding Ollie's hand as he explained the differences between US and UK road signs to her dad, who was amiably asking questions. He met Polly's eye in the rear-view mirror and winked at her. *We're here and we're going to have a great time. I know it.*

"How's the farm, Dad?" she asked.

"It's going great," her father said warmly. "We installed the heat pump a few weeks back, and the turbine has been fantastic. We're generating most of our own electricity already, and we're only halfway through installing the solar panels."

"What about the store?" This was the part of her dad's farm project that Polly was most interested in. "The buildings you were going to convert so you could sell organic produce and recycled goods? And maybe my clothes?"

She had brought a trunkful of her favourite designs, all carefully folded in crinkling tissue paper. Dresses and skirts, scarves and jewellery, all upcycled and adapted for her label Turned Around With Love. She and Ollie had been selling them in the Heartside Bay market all summer, and the success of their stall had bought their plane tickets. Would Turned Around With Love work as well over here as it had worked at home?

"The store is already getting customers," said her father. He turned off the highway on to a road that dipped away among warm green hills. "I have a whole area sectioned off for your fashion, Polly. I hope you've brought plenty of stock to sell."

"Two trunks' worth," Ollie said, smiling proudly at Polly. "I had to leave my football behind so we could fit everything in."

"Polly mentioned you play soccer. Are you in training now?" asked Polly's dad with interest.

Polly listened to her dad and her boyfriend discussing football – or soccer, as they called it over here. She loved the way Ollie's face lit up when he was talking about his favourite game. He could talk for hours on the subject of football. While she didn't exactly understand the appeal of running around a field after a little ball, she liked watching Ollie's face when he was talking about it. And she was happy to see her dad and Ollie chatting so easily.

"We'll try and find a ball next time we're in town so we can have a few kickabouts in the yard," Polly's dad said. "But I should warn you, the farm is twenty minutes from any town big enough to sell a soccer ball."

"I'll try to soldier through," said Ollie, putting on a long-suffering face. Polly shoved his arm gently and he broke out in a grin. "I think I can take a week off of football if it means I get to spend time in California with you," he whispered in her ear.

Polly's dad flicked on his indicator and turned through a wide wooden gate marked *Paradise Farm*. Polly noted the board that stood propped against the side of the road, advertising the farm store. *Coming soon to Paradise Farm: UK fashion eco-brand Turned Around With Love.* Her stomach gave a little flip of excitement to see it. If she could sell all the stock that she had brought, her trip would pay for itself all over again.

"I have plenty of chores for you both this week," said her father, interrupting Polly's daydream. "A biodynamic farm doesn't run itself. You can both work in the store, muck out the horses, help pick some of the produce, that kind of thing."

"Sounds great," Ollie enthused. "I've never been on a working farm before. What animals do you have?"

"At the moment we have some cows, a few pigs, a load of chickens and a goat. All our animals are rescue animals, saved either from factory farms or abusive owners. We give them a place to live out in the fresh air. Some of them had never even walked on grass before coming to us. They'd spent their whole lives cooped up in some overcrowded prison of a farm." He shook his head sadly. "Hold up a second."

He pulled the station wagon up beside a tin mailbox on a wooden post and flipped down the little tin door to collect the post. Then they drove on again.

The little road was growing steeper now, wending through green pastures. Polly glimpsed the silver twist of the river down in the valley below, while a wind turbine marked the top of the hill.

As they turned one last corner, the farmhouse came into view, all red-painted weatherboarding and a wide veranda angled to catch the morning sun. Outbuildings of local stone and wood stood haphazardly around a central yard. A solitary brown cow gazed enquiringly over the fence beside the farmhouse, as if to welcome them all.

Polly felt a moment of pure happiness as her father

brought the station wagon to halt in the yard. They were here, the sun was shining, Ollie was beside her and she had a whole week of her dad's undivided attention. She already knew this was going to be the best week of her life.

As she climbed out of the back seat, Polly glimpsed a beautiful woman with a girl about Polly's age. Customers for the store, she guessed. They both had long, thick blonde hair and sun-kissed skin. They were wearing tight-fitting jeans and slim-cut shirts that screamed designer.

Welcome to California, Polly thought wryly. She tugged at the back of her skirt, which had crumpled against the backs of her legs on the journey. Her skin felt paler than ever, as if she'd spent half her life under a stone. She wished she'd dyed her hair a sharper, brighter shade of blonde. Next to those two, she felt dull.

Her dad hopped out of the car, busying himself with the cases in the boot. Polly's good mood dampened slightly as she watched the two women. They were unnaturally gorgeous, sunshine gleaming on their perfect hair. One of them threw her head back and laughed, flashing a perfect set of Hollywood teeth. She looked at Ollie, who was also glancing over at the women. She felt a stab of jealousy. Polly hated how insecure she sometimes got around other girls. She tried telling herself that she was cute and stylish and fun when she was at home, looking in the mirror, but as soon as she found herself standing next to tall leggy girls with flowing hair she couldn't help feeling stumpy and boring. She shook her head trying to dislodge her thoughts.

"No one is born with teeth like that," she whispered to Ollie.

"They are a bit high wattage," Ollie laughed.

Polly relaxed as he leaned down to give a quick kiss on the cheek.

The taller of the two blondes had seen the car. Waving and running across the yard in long loping strides, her hair bouncing prettily on her shoulders, she threw her arms around Polly's dad and gave him a kiss that was best described as passionate. Polly blinked.

Talk about customer service, she thought. What was going on?

The woman finally broke away.

"You must be Polly!" she said, flashing her brilliant teeth in Polly's direction. "Alex, you wretch. You never told me how pretty your daughter is!"

Polly's dad was looking uncomfortable. The woman chattered on, oblivious.

"Oh, forgive my manners! I haven't introduced myself. I'm Courtney, your dad's girlfriend. I'm so happy to meet you at last!"

FOUR

Polly felt her mind freeze. Her dad had a *girlfriend*? *What*? Not once, in all the conversations they'd had about her trip over to San Francisco, had he mentioned a girlfriend. She felt a terrible urge to scream with shock and disappointment. *There goes our father-daughter holiday*, she thought.

"Um, hello," she managed as Courtney beamed at her.

Polly's father extracted himself from his girlfriend's arms and hugged Polly awkwardly.

"Give Courtney and Willow a chance, Pollydolly," he whispered into her ear. He sounded tense. "For your old dad, OK?"

Willow? Polly thought, feeling more disorientated

than ever. "Who or what is a Willow?" she asked, a little too loudly.

The blonde girl standing behind Courtney gave a little wave with the tips of her French-manicured fingers. "That's me!" she said brightly. "Hey, Polly. I'm sure we're going to be like sisters."

The girl sauntered around to Polly's father and looped her arm around his waist. Polly found herself biting her lip as her dad planted a kiss on this pretty stranger's forehead.

"We're going to have so much fun on the farm!" said Willow with a giggle. "I'll show you to your room, OK? It's right next to mine. We'll practically be roomies!"

Polly's already unsteady world tilted a little further on its axis.

"You live here?" she said, aghast. Why hadn't her father warned her about any of this?

"We sure do," said Courtney. She seemed oblivious to the tension in the air as she fluttered her long eyelashes at Ollie. "Won't you introduce us to the lovely hunk on your arm, Polly?"

Belatedly, Polly remembered Ollie, who was hanging around discreetly beside the car. "Um, sure," she said, trying to organize her head. *Willow and Courtney lived with her dad.* "This is Ollie."

Ollie politely shook hands with Courtney and Willow. "It's really nice to meet you," he said.

Willow gave a little squeal. "Your accent is so cute!" she gasped, shaking Ollie's hand for a lot longer than Polly liked. "Did you hear that, Mom?"

"Believe me honey, I did," said Courtney. She winked at Ollie.

Ollie grinned, enjoying the attention.

"Say something else," Willow begged, her eyes shining. To Polly's horror, she was stroking her fingers up Ollie's arm. "I could listen to you all day."

"You look like a Californian already, Ollie," put in Courtney. "All you need is the tan."

Ollie was expanding like a flower in the sunshine with all the female attention. "A week in this place will sort that out," he said, smiling broadly. "I'll be blending with the natives before you can say London Bridge."

Even her dad started grinning as Willow squealed again. Polly gritted her teeth. *Tanning isn't even good for you*, was all she could think.

She could picture the scene already. Her hiding miserably under a beach umbrella, and Ollie all brown and muscled, his hair almost white from the sun, playing volleyball with Willow and her equally beautiful friends to the sound of the crashing Californian surf. The image was so strong, Polly felt quite faint with jealousy.

"I'm really tired," she said abruptly. "It was a long flight."

Willow stopped giggling and pawing Ollie and turned her wide, concerned blue eyes in Polly's direction. "Of course you're tired, how thoughtless of me," she said. "You could probably use a nap right now, couldn't you? What time is it back in the UK?"

Time I wasn't here, Polly thought. "About two a.m.," she said out loud.

"Goodness, no wonder you look so pale," said Willow blithely.

The girl probably meant to sound sympathetic, but her words made Polly feel more like a slug than ever.

"Alex, honey," said Courtney, linking arms with Polly's dad again and smiling warmly into his eyes, "Are Polly and Ollie's rooms ready?"

Polly wanted to jump in between her dad and this woman and prise them apart. Courtney was acting like she owned this place. Like she owned Polly's dad.

"They sure are, Mom," Willow said brightly. "I made the beds specially this morning. Follow me, Polly, I'll show you where you're sleeping."

Willow was as bad as her mother, taking charge like a perfect hostess. *I want my dad to show me the farmhouse,* Polly wanted to shout. But her dad and Ollie were laughing about something Courtney was saying. Polly felt utterly excluded.

"Ollie?" she said beseechingly. "Are you coming?"

Ollie turned round. "Your dad said he'd show me the barn. This place is so cool. Why don't you take a nap and I'll see you later?"

"Are you coming, Polly?" Willow said, one foot on the steps that led up to the veranda and the big front door of the farmhouse.

Polly tore her eyes away from Ollie and her dad. "Whatever," she muttered.

She knew she sounded sullen, but she couldn't help it. This wasn't how it was supposed to be. She and Ollie were supposed to have her father and the farm all to themselves. With these two around, she was as good as invisible.

She heaved her suitcase up the steps after Willow to the sound of Ollie's laughter echoing around the farmyard behind her. It felt like the whole holiday was ruined before it had even begun.

FIVE

When she woke up, it took several moments for Polly to work out where she was. She blinked at the unfamiliar ceiling with its woven rattan lampshade, her eyelids heavy with sleep and confusion. Light was pouring through the chink in the blue-and-white striped linen curtains that hung at the bedroom window, and outside were sounds that didn't feature on an average morning in Heartside Bay. Clucking, and mooing, and the call of a bird that she didn't recognize.

She sat bolt upright as she remembered. She was in California! A thrill of excitement rushed through her. Yesterday seemed like a jet-lagged dream: the strange way that she'd felt on meeting Courtney and Willow, the sense of being left out. She had nothing to be jealous of. Ollie had proved that to her last night, as he had walked with her around the farmhouse after dinner and kissed her softly in the moonlight by the barn.

I won't let Courtney and Willow ruin this week, Polly vowed to herself. *I'm going to enjoy myself.*

She checked her phone for the time. Ten o'clock in the morning. That equated to six p.m. in Heartside Bay. If she was at home, she would have packed up her stall by now, banked her takings and headed to the Heartbeat Café for a drink with Ollie and their friends. It was strange, picturing Lila, Rhi and Eve hanging out back in England without her.

She took a long shower in a vast bathroom just down the corridor from her room. Everything in the farmhouse was quiet, save the sound of a ticking grandfather clock down in the hall. Polly took extra care with her clothes, selecting an outfit she had designed especially for this trip: a forest-green dress with a white Peter Pan collar and cuffs that she'd transferred from a vintage blouse. She knew that the colour of the dress brought out the green in her hazel eyes. With sandals on her feet and her hair loose around her shoulders, she was satisfied. She applied a dab of lipgloss and headed downstairs in search of breakfast and company.

"Hello?" she called, moving through the farmhouse, peering around doors. "Anybody here?"

The grandfather clock ticked steadily on. Trying to quash the uncomfortable feeling of being left out all over again, Polly found some bread and jam in the kitchen and washed it down with a glass of fresh orange juice. The silence of the farmhouse was beginning to unnerve her.

"You must show us your designs!" Courtney had enthused over dinner the night before. "I'm sure they're going to be just darling!"

"Polly's really talented," Ollie had said warmly.

Polly had made herself smile. She wanted to press all her tops and skirts and dresses, and make sure they were one hundred per cent perfect before Courtney and Willow saw them. "You can see them tomorrow," she'd said, and changed the subject.

It was soothing now, taking the dresses out of their tissue beds and shaking them out, opening the jewellery boxes and straightening the seashell necklaces that she'd brought with her. Carrying an armful of her best items back down the stairs, Polly hunted out a steam iron and ironing board in the kitchen and set to work, smoothing out the travel creases and hanging the items on the adorable wooden hangers she'd brought especially for the store, that she'd hand-painted with her Turned Around With Love button logo.

Her father had taken her and Ollie around the store after dinner the night before, proudly showing them the area he'd earmarked specially for Polly's fashions. Polly could already picture her dresses and skirts and jewellery and hair ornaments filling the fresh and airy space, ready to dazzle the Californian customers. Suddenly she couldn't wait to get started.

Hearing voices outside, Polly scooped up an armful of her favourite designs and headed down the veranda steps into the farmyard, to find someone to show them to. She stopped for a moment with the sun on her face, enjoying the warmth and the fresh smells: earth, animals, straw, wood and plants. Everything was so beautiful and lush. As Polly wandered among the rows of green vegetables and the fruit in the orchard, she spotted beans, and carrots, and peas.

A contented-looking goat watched her from a shady pen, and two cows stood together in a lush pasture, grazing idly. Looping the dresses over one arm, she stroked the fruit dangling temptingly from the branches until her fingers were scented with peach and lemon. Flowers grew in profusion too: lilies, and lavender, and brightly coloured sturdy little plants she couldn't name.

Walking through the vegetable garden, past the animals and through the orchard, brought her back to the farmyard. A few chickens scratched and basked in the dust, fluffing out their feathers for extra warmth. It made her happy to see all the animals enjoying the sun and fresh air.

Looking past the chickens, she saw the stone barn ahead. Her dad had shown her and Ollie around this part of the farm the previous evening. She followed the line of outbuildings until she reached the big stone barn which housed the shop.

She went in through the distinctive red doors. Inside it was cool and airy. Vegetables and fruit were displayed in natural woven baskets, freezers filled with ice cream and organic frozen treats winked at the back of the barn, eggs from the sunbathing chickens nestled in straw-filled baskets. The rails stood empty, ready for her clothes.

Polly let her eyes adjust to the dimness, and saw her dad across by the freezers. She lifted her hand to wave – and dropped it in horror. Her father wasn't alone. He was kissing Courtney.

All the optimism of her morning crumbled, replaced once again with awful feelings of uncertainty. Did her dad even want her here this week? Once again, Polly felt like a guest in her own life.

As she backed towards the barn doors, her face aflame, she prayed her dad and Courtney hadn't seen her come in. Safely outside, she leaned on the warm stone of the barn wall, holding her precious designs against herself, tipping her face to the light and trying not to cry. *I need Ollie*, was the only clear thought in her head. *He'll make me feel better about Dad and Courtney.*

She walked back across the farmyard, looking in the outbuildings, hunting for Ollie. He had to be here *somewhere*. He couldn't just vanish.

At last, from the final outbuilding in the corner of

the yard, Polly heard laughter. Following the sound, she entered the dim cow-smelling space.

Willow was giggling helplessly, her arms wrapped around Ollie.

"You're so bad at this!" she trilled, laying her hands on Ollie's fingers as he pulled haplessly at the udder of a patiently chewing brown cow.

"I thought I was doing pretty well," Ollie protested, laughing almost as much as Willow. Even in the dim light of the cow barn, his cheeks looked flushed. "Look, there's a whole squirt of milk in the bucket."

Willow made her eyes look bigger and rounder than ever. "Hey, maybe we should enter you in a contest for making the world's smallest cheese. You'd win the prize for sure." And she ran the back of her hand along Ollie's strong brown forearm.

Not Ollie too.

Willow had a massive crush on Ollie, anyone could see that. How did Ollie feel about her? She was beautiful, outgoing, friendly. *Way* too friendly. Polly wished she knew the answer. She hurried backwards, reaching for the door. She was unwanted everywhere she went.

"Oh!" she gasped, catching her foot on an uneven floorboard as she reached the barn door. As Willow and Ollie looked round, Polly flailed to keep her balance, trying not to drop the armful of clothes she had so carefully pressed and ironed that morning. *Don't fall over*, she thought in anguish. *Not in front of Willow. Not in front of. . .*

CRASH.

The wired edge of the chicken pen outside the doors bowed and gave way, and Polly fell bottom first into the pen among the squawking feathers and landed with a bump in the dust.

SIX

Polly's whole body was burning with embarrassment. She struggled to her feet, frantically brushing at her dress, which was covered in chicken muck and straw. Her beautiful designs lay in a crushed heap among the hens as they ran from side to side around her feet, squawking fit to burst. Several chickens had already escaped through the downed section of wire, and were pecking around the farmyard.

"Polly!" Ollie ran from the cow barn, Willow close behind. "Hey, what happened? Are you OK?"

Her father and Courtney emerged from the store barn now to see what the noise was about. Meanwhile, Willow with her hands pressed across her mouth, stifling fits of silent laughter.

"I'm fine," she muttered. "I just . . . it's my fault, I

caught my foot. . ." *I saw Willow holding you in her arms. I'm so embarrassed. Why does this kind of thing always happen to me?*

Ollie pulled her into a hug, brushing the straw and dirt off her dress. Her beautiful, specially designed dress. "Whoa, that was a nasty fall. You're lucky you didn't bang your head," he said, pushing her mussed-up hair out of her eyes.

Polly felt numb with humiliation. She couldn't bear to look at her carefully ironed designs as they lay in a sorry tangle among the straw in the broken pen. Instead she held on to Ollie and wished herself a thousand miles away from everywhere. "I'm sorry," she said hopelessly as chickens darted across the yard in a blur of brown feathers.

Courtney and Willow both started trying to round up the escaped hens.

"Don't worry about it, Pollydolly," said her dad warmly. "Catching chickens is fun."

Ollie kissed her on the forehead. "Everything in this place is fun," he said, his voice brimming with enthusiasm. "I've been feeding chickens and milking a cow. I even drove the tractor this morning!"

He *had* been busy. Willow had probably been busy too, right alongside him.

"Why didn't you wake me up?" Polly asked, feeling forlorn.

"You were pretty tired yesterday. Willow suggested leaving you to sleep in."

Polly felt more upset than ever. *I bet she did. I bet she really enjoyed having you all to herself this morning.*

Ollie tipped her face to look up at him. "Are you sure you're OK?"

His eyes were so honest and so blue and he was looking at her with such concern. Polly swallowed. "My pride took a bit of a battering, that's all," she said, fighting back the tears. "And my . . . my clothes. . ."

She looked sadly at the tangle of fabric lying in the chicken pen. Her designs had been so beautiful when she had ironed them that morning and hung them on their pretty painted hangers.

Willow had successfully captured a chicken, and was bringing it back to the pen while her mother and Polly's dad attempted to catch the rest.

"What's with the rags?" she said, nodding at the clothes in the pen. The captured chicken squawked

43

under her arm. "Did you bring them over from England to donate to one of our local charities?"

Polly felt worse than ever. What was she supposed to say to that?

"These are Polly's designs for the store," Ollie said, bending down to pick up the clothes and hangers. "They'll be fine," he assured Polly. "It's just a bit of dust. I'm sure it'll all brush out."

"Polly's designs are a big hit in the UK," said her dad, returning the other escaped chickens to the pen and yanking up the wire netting to secure the birds again. "They fit perfectly with our organic ethos here on the farm."

"We almost sold out of dresses on our market stall this summer," Ollie said. "If it hadn't been for Polly's designs, we could never have flown the whole way out to San Francisco to join you guys."

Polly felt exhausted and sad and humiliated all at once. Her dad and Ollie were trying to help, but the sting of Willow's comments wouldn't go away. She wished she could spirit Ollie out of this place, and take him back to England. They could forget this trip had ever happened.

"Sorry," said Willow, having the grace to look embarrassed. "I didn't realize."

Courtney took one of the least crumpled items out of Ollie's arms and shook it out, holding it up so that the sunlight poured through the fine printed cotton. "Adorable," she said doubtfully. "I'm sure they'll be a real hit with our customers. There's something so special about the eccentric English style."

Willow gazed at the dress Polly was wearing. She eyed the cuffs, one of which had ripped away from the dress on impact with the chicken wire. "Fashion sure is different in England," she said.

Polly summoned a scrap of strength from somewhere. *I won't let Courtney and Willow see how much their comments hurt*, she thought. *I won't let them win.* She'd learned a lot from surviving years of abuse from when her friend Eve was in her evil phase. She could handle these two.

"There's a lot you won't understand about English fashion," she said as pleasantly as she could. "Why would you? You're American."

The look on Willow's face made her feel better at once. *Two can play at this game*, she thought, her confidence creeping back. *I won't let you walk all over me.*

The chickens started squawking again as a truck rumbled up the road towards the farmyard, followed by several cars. Polly's dad looked alert.

"I've been expecting those guys in the truck for the past hour," he said. "We have a big order for an organic restaurant in the city. They only use our fruit and vegetables," he added, sounding proud. "Courtney, could you help Polly with her clothes? They only got a little dusty, I'm sure we can still hang them in the store. The other cars will be customers, I expect."

As Polly's dad broke into a little jog, waving at the drivers of the truck, Courtney gingerly took the clothes from Ollie's arms. "We'll hang these up right away," she said. "I'm sure they'll look as good as new on the rails."

"They aren't new," Ollie pointed out. "They're recycled."

Polly felt a giggle rising in her throat as Courtney carried her designs towards the store. Good old Ollie. He really was there to support her.

Willow sidled up and slipped her brown hand through the crook of Ollie's elbow. "Ready for the rest of your farm tour?" she asked, looking at Ollie through her thick eyelashes. "I'm your own personal tour guide for the morning."

Oh no you don't, Polly thought.

"Ollie, could you come here for a moment?" she asked sweetly.

Ollie disentangled himself from Willow's grasp and bounded over to Polly.

"What's up Polls?" he asked.

"I missed you this morning," she whispered into his ear, and then pulled his face to hers and kissed him soundly. After a second of surprise, Ollie reacted with enthusiasm, wrapping his hands around her waist and lifting her up.

When Ollie set her back on the dusty ground again, Polly snuck a glance at Willow and was pleased to see that she was frowning.

"Actually, Willow, I'd like to explore the farm with my boyfriend. You don't mind, do you? You'd better get back to your milking anyway, hadn't you?" she said, putting her arm around Ollie's waist.

SEVEN

Exploring the farm was a lot more fun with Ollie. Polly felt herself expanding with the sunlight, the warmth and the excitement of each discovery – barns, fields, woodpiles – like the flowers growing in profusion around the edges of the paths and pastureland. Organic farming was so special, the way everything grew in such harmony. No weedkillers, no artificial pesticides. Just bees and beetles flying peacefully about their business, crops waving in the fields and the warm smell of earth and flowers everywhere you turned. If only life could be so harmonious.

Ollie picked a handful of large daisies growing on the wayside and pressed them into Polly's hands. "For you," he said, smiling.

Polly bent her nose to the flowers and inhaled their warm, dusty smell. Ollie could be really romantic when he wanted to be. "Do you think it was horrible of me to say what I said to Willow?" she asked, peeping up at him through the petals.

"Yes," said Ollie, idly swiping at the tall grasses that lined the path they were walking along.

Polly felt anxious. "Really?"

He laughed and rubbed her head with the palm of his hand. "Of course not! You're so easy to tease, Polly Nelson."

"She didn't look too pleased," Polly said, smiling a little guiltily at the memory.

"It's really tough being told you can't spend time with someone as good-looking as me," Ollie said with an exaggerated sigh.

Polly whacked him, laughing. "Your head is as big as the watermelons Dad is growing by the side of the cow barn."

Ollie caught her around the waist. "Say that again!"

Polly wriggled away from Ollie and made a dash across the middle of a nearby field. A small brown cow watched impassively as Ollie gave chase.

"You're not getting away that easily," he said, catching her around the waist, picking her up and kissing her neck.

"Mind my flowers!"

Ollie put Polly down with exaggerated gentleness. "These daisies were very expensive," he said seriously, stroking Polly's hair back from her face. His touch made her feel breathless. "In fact, they are the only such flowers in existence."

"Apart from the million other daisies growing on the path," Polly pointed out.

Ollie raised a finger. "Those are completely *different* daisies." He ran his finger down her cheek and under her chin. "Those are *common* daisies."

Polly stood on tiptoe and kissed Ollie lightly on the lips.

"My daisies are beautiful," she said, looking into his warm blue eyes.

"So are you."

The morning slipped away like silk, every moment feeling more enchanted than the last. They played hide and seek in the orchard, rewarding each other with peaches and kisses. They lay among long grasses in the fields watching wispy clouds scud through the blue sky, and climbed a gnarly oak to the topmost branches, marvelling at the view across the valley, all the way out to the Pacific Ocean glinting in the far distance. They laughed, and kissed, and laughed some more, and Polly forgot all her woes.

She slid her hand into his warm palm as they walked slowly back towards the farmyard and the house, tired and happy. "Let's see if there are any eggs in the chicken pen," she said.

Back in the farmyard, the chickens had recovered from their shocks of the morning and were scratching about contentedly. There was no sign of Willow in the cow barn.

"I hope she's OK," said Polly, feeling a little guilty. "I really wasn't very nice to her this morning."

"I'm sure she's fine," Ollie soothed. "You don't have to worry about other people all the time, Polly."

Polly couldn't help it. It was in her nature. *Willow probably hates me even more now*, she thought gloomily.

"Eggs?" Ollie prompted, opening the gate to the chicken pen.

Polly peered inside the hens' spacious nesting boxes. Bright eyes gazed out at her. Leaving the few nesting hens alone, she hunted through the clean fresh straw of the empty boxes. After five or six attempts, she found something.

"An egg!" she crowed, wriggling out and holding her prize aloft.

"It's hardly going to be anything else, is it?" Ollie replied, looking amused.

Polly set the egg and her flowers carefully down on top of the farm wall. "You could have it for breakfast tomorrow," she said. "Oh!"

The egg had already rolled off the wall and plopped on to the hard packed earth of the yard with a splat. Ollie laughed uproariously.

"Oh," said Polly again, feeling crestfallen. What an idiot. Everyone knew that eggs rolled.

She glanced up at a sudden movement behind one of the curtains in the house, a flick of blonde hair and the flash of an eye. It looked like Willow was watching them.

"There'll be other eggs," Ollie laughed, drawing her attention back to him. He tugged her towards the hay barn. "Let's see what's up here."

The barn was lofty and still, the air full of dancing motes of straw and dust. Ollie made a beeline for the stack of hay bales piled in one corner like a giant jigsaw puzzle. He started scaling the dusty blocks, leaping lightly from one to the other, and was near the top of the barn before Polly had fully adjusted her eyes to the dim light.

"I'm the King of the Castle!" he shouted, flexing his muscles. His voice echoed around the barn, causing birds to flap away from the eaves in alarm. "Come up here, Poll, it's amazing. Like a giant playground!"

He seemed to fall backwards and disappear.

"Ollie?" Polly climbed up, trying to spot his red shirt through the gaps in the bales. "Where did you go?"

Ollie was two bales below, grinning at her, his hands behind his head as he sprawled full-length in the soft pale-yellow hay. "You took your time," he said.

He looked so gorgeous lying there, all lean and long, tanned and muscled and blond. Was he really her boyfriend? Polly still found it hard to believe that Ollie was hers.

Flinging her arms up to the roof, she jumped down with a squeal to join him.

"You have almost as much hay in your hair as me," he commented, reaching up to pluck a stem of dried grass from behind her ear. He drew her closer, wrapped his arms around her and kissed her. Time seemed to stand still. It was just her and Ollie, the smell of the straw and the feel of his lips on hers.

I could get used to country life, Polly thought dimly.

"Stand up, right now!"

The shout made Polly jump out of her skin. She scrambled away from Ollie, looking upwards – to where her father was standing on the bales, his hands on his hips and a look of pure fury on his face as he gazed down on the incriminating scene. Ollie went pale.

"Dad?" Polly gasped. Her hands went to her hair. She was more covered in hay than ever. *What must I look like?*

"On your feet!" her dad yelled again, even louder than before. "Out of there, both of you!"

"I'm really sorry, sir," Ollie stammered, red-faced and horrified as he scrambled to his feet, ineffectually brushing the hay off his shirt, helping Polly upright.

54

Polly found that her legs were trembling like jelly. "I swear, it's not what it looks like—"

"I wasn't born yesterday," interrupted Polly's father coldly. "I had hoped you would treat my daughter with more respect than this." He switched his gaze to Polly. "I can't believe you would act this way, Polly. Poor Willow was very hurt when you two went off without her this morning. She came crying to me about it just ten minutes ago. And now this?"

The twitching curtain, the flash of blonde hair. . . Polly felt a rush of anger. *Poor Willow* indeed. She had a fair idea who had told her father where he would find her and Ollie.

Blushing and stammering, Ollie helped Polly down from the bales. "Really sir, I can't apologize enough. . ."

"Keep trying," snarled Polly's dad as they reached the barn floor.

Polly needed to get a grip on the situation. "Dad," she said as calmly as she could, still trying to pull straw from her hair, "can we talk about this?"

"We'll talk about it right now." He levelled an accusing finger at Ollie. "I'll deal with you later, young man. Polly, you come with me."

Polly exchanged glances with Ollie, and followed her dad out of the barn.

"I am so embarrassed," her father hissed, the moment they reached the sunlit yard. "Is this how your mother raised you? To sneak off with boys?"

Polly stared at her dad's angry face. It was a face she used to know so well, but now – she didn't think she knew it at all. *None of this was fair.*

"You're one to talk," she said angrily.

Her father blinked, thrown by Polly's direct challenge. "What do you mean? I'm not the one who's been doing heaven knows what in a hay barn!"

He wasn't getting off the hook that easily. Polly felt cold and furious. He couldn't accuse her like this! Not when there were questions he needed to answer first.

"Why didn't you tell me about Courtney and Willow?" All her uncertainty about the events of the past twenty-four hours came tumbling out as rage, loud and aggressive. "Do you have any idea how yesterday felt for me? How today has felt?"

Her dad looked shocked. "It's not the same thing, Polly. I'm your *father*."

"From where I'm standing, you look more like Willow's," Polly said coldly. "You've replaced me and Mum now. I come to visit and find two total strangers living with you: your new, perfect, *secret* family! No explanation, no warning, nothing. How could you have done something like this without telling me? Answer me that!"

EIGHT

Polly's dad looked abashed.

"I'm sorry," he said after a moment. All the anger seemed to have gone out of him, as if he'd forgotten about Ollie entirely. "Maybe this was a bad idea."

Polly froze. He was regretting inviting her and Ollie to California. He was wishing his life could just be with his new family on his beautiful farm, far away from her and her anxieties. She felt panicky, like a bird trapped in a cage.

Her father sighed. "I should have told you about Courtney and Willow. I thought maybe, by doing it this way, it would somehow be easier. It all happened so fast, you see. There seemed no point in telling you on the phone when you guys could just meet and. . . Well. Get along, I thought. I hoped."

Polly wanted to take back everything she'd just said. Why hadn't she kept her mouth shut? She loved her dad. She didn't want him to think that she didn't. *She didn't want to lose him again.*

"I'm still your dad, Polly," he said gently, interrupting her chaotic, whirling thoughts. "I'm sorry it hasn't seemed that way over the past few days. You're my daughter, and I love you. Nothing will ever change that. Not Courtney, not Willow."

Polly felt swamped with relief. Her emotions were all over the place at the moment: high one moment and low the next. If she let herself think about it too hard, she would probably cry and be completely unable to stop. She nodded wordlessly, swallowing the tears that were balling at the back of her throat.

Her father studied her face. "Your young man back in the barn," he said. "I hope you're taking things slowly, honey."

Polly flushed, embarrassed all over again. *I don't want this conversation*, she thought wearily. In many ways, she felt that her dad had lost the right to tell her what to do the day he had left their lives.

"I've loved Ollie for a long time, Dad," she said.

"You're still very young," her father began.

Polly interrupted him. "I'm not nine any more," she said. She tried to smile at him. "A lot changes in six years, Dad."

She could see her dad flinch. *Six years when you weren't in my life*, she thought. She knew he was thinking it too.

"I'm fifteen now, and I know what I'm doing," she went on. "I am being careful, but Ollie is a good guy, Dad. He's always been respectful towards me, he looks out for me. He gave me this when we first started seeing each other."

Feeling under the collar of her dress, she carefully pulled out her locket on its long chain, and showed it to her father. The Californian sun shone on the gleaming silver, picking out what remained of her etched initials.

"That's very nice," said her father. "But—"

My life, my rules, Polly thought. "You have to trust me. And I'd like you to get along with Ollie, Dad," she interrupted. "You owe me that much. I can't handle any more conflict in my family."

For a moment, Polly could see tears sparkling in her father's eyes.

"You really have grown up, haven't you Polly?" he said. "You've become a beautiful young woman, and I never even realized. I'm sorry I missed so much." He rubbed his forehead. "Forgive me, honey. It's not easy seeing your little girl in the arms of a boyfriend for the first time."

"I'm not a little girl now," Polly said, tucking her locket away again and touching her father's hand.

"You'll always be *my* little girl," her father said, half smiling. "But I'll try and remember that you see things a little differently these days. I'm sorry I went a bit Dadzilla back there. I hope Ollie will forgive me."

"He will," Polly said, gladness welling up in her heart. "He's the forgiving type."

Her father hugged her tightly. "Hey," he said, releasing her, "why don't the three of us head into San Francisco on our own tomorrow? I could get to know Ollie better. We could all spend some real quality time together. What do you say?"

Polly allowed herself to picture it. The tall buildings, the glittering bay. The cable cars, the hills, the museums, the shops. Memories to share with her dad, places to show Ollie. No Courtney. No Willow making cow eyes at Ollie's muscles. "That would be perfect," she said, unable to put into words just *how* perfect.

"Great! We have a date." Her father eyed the barn. "But I guess I'd better go test out your theory about Ollie's forgiving nature first. Right?"

At dinner, Ollie looked so dismayed at his plate of food that Polly almost giggled.

"Um," he said, "can I ask what this is?"

Courtney bustled out of the kitchen in a spotless striped apron, holding a large dish of something brown and dry-looking. "Kale and tofu with coconut oil," she said, setting the dish down in the middle of the round pine table where Polly, her dad, Ollie and Willow were all sitting. "It has so many healthful properties."

Ollie poked doubtfully at the shrivel of greenery perched on his plate. "There isn't very much of it, is there?" he tried.

Tonight Courtney's hair had been caught up on her

head in a perfect French plait. "That's not all we're having, silly," she teased, trilling with laughter.

Ollie looked relieved.

"Help yourself to spiced quinoa," she went on, pushing the bowl of grain across the table towards him. "It's simply packed with iron, lycine and magnesium."

Polly was a vegetarian, so the dish actually sounded pretty good to her. But she could see that for Ollie, the ingredients sounded like a bad chemistry experiment.

"Is there a little meat to go with the, uh, quinoa?" he said hopefully.

Courtney sucked her teeth in disapproval. "Quinoa is one of the most protein-rich foods you can have, Ollie. Meat is so *unnecessary*."

Willow was already helping herself, spooning the brown quinoa daintily on the side of her plate. Polly took up her fork and dug into the crispy kale. She choked lightly, covering her mouth with her fingers. It was so dry and bland. She exchanged a look with Ollie.

"I don't suppose there's any ketchup?" Ollie said, looking beseechingly at Polly's dad.

"You'll find the ketchup in the fridge," Polly's dad

replied, forking through his quinoa and kale dinner. He made Polly think of an archaeologist digging for remains. "I wouldn't mind a little myself."

Courtney looked more disapproving than ever as Ollie returned to the table with a bottle of ketchup, which he squirted liberally over his plate.

"So," said Polly's dad as the sound of eating filled the kitchen. "We were thinking of going to San Francisco tomorrow."

Courtney clapped her hands. "What a terrific idea, baby!" she beamed. "San Francisco has such a great vibe. We'll all have so much fun together!"

"I want to go shopping," Willow piped up.

Polly tensed. *Please, not Courtney and Willow too.*

"Actually, I was thinking of taking Polly and Ollie on their own," Polly's dad said, to her acute relief. "Polly and I have a lot of catching up to do, and I need a chance to get to know the boy who has my daughter's heart."

Polly could see that neither Willow nor Courtney liked the idea. Courtney's glossy lips pursed. "If that's the way you feel," she said in a tight voice, "then I guess Willow and I will just stay home. I just thought it would be fun together."

Polly's dad took Courtney's hand across the table. "It's just one day, honey," he said. "We'll all go to the beach together later in the week. You'll like that, won't you?"

Courtney stiffly forked up a frond of kale and put it between her lips. She looked like she was chewing a wasp. The rest of the meal continued in frosty silence. No one was eating much of Courtney's quinoa dish, not even Willow.

After a bowl of peaches warm from the orchard, Courtney announced that she was going to bed.

"We women have to look after our skins, don't we Polly?" she said, eyeing Polly's sun-reddened cheeks. "A good night's sleep can work wonders."

Willow wasn't far behind her mother in leaving the table. Then it was just Polly, Ollie and her dad. The atmosphere lightened almost at once. Ollie's stomach rumbled loudly.

"You took the words right out of my mouth, son." Polly's dad pushed back his chair. "Who's for more food?"

"I am so glad your dad said that," Ollie muttered

as they followed Polly's father into the kitchen. "Otherwise I might have had to break into the fridge myself."

"Anyone for a peanut butter and jam sandwich?" Polly's father enquired. "They used to be Polly's favourite when she was a kid. I think I have a jar in here somewhere. Courtney doesn't like to buy anything with added salt and sugar, but when it comes to peanut butter the all-natural stuff just doesn't taste the same. So I keep a secret stash." He winked conspiratorially at Polly.

Polly sighed in satisfaction as she tucked into her sandwich. She grinned at the bliss on Ollie's face as he took the first huge bite of his own.

"You are my hero, Alex," Ollie announced, as they sat on the darkening veranda after clearing up and watched the bright stars in the dark, velvety sky. "I might have to take a jar of that peanut butter back to Heartside with me. And that plum jam was like nothing I've ever tasted before."

"The taste of Paradise," said Polly's dad, looking proud. "To be more specific, Paradise Farm. We grow the plums just over there," he said, pointing vaguely.

Polly's tummy was full of sweet jam, melty peanut

butter and soft brown bread. She closed her eyes and rested her head on Ollie's shoulder, listening to her boyfriend and her dad talking and laughing together. It was great that they were getting along so well. The embarrassing incident in the barn earlier that day felt as if it had never happened.

San Francisco tomorrow was going to be epic.

At least, she hoped so.

NINE

"We are going to have such a great day," Polly said enthusiastically as the first signs of the city crept on to the horizon. She waved the guidebook she'd bought. "There are some incredible art galleries I would love to see."

Ollie looked wary. "Art galleries? I thought we were going to Alcatraz?"

"We can do both," remarked Polly's dad. He slid on his indicator. "You guys will just have to sort out the details between you."

"The museums are really amazing, Ollie," said Polly pleadingly. "There's this beautiful one in Golden Gate Park called the de Young Museum. It has an incredible collection of textile art that I'd really like to see."

Ollie stuck out his bottom lip. "I want to see Alcatraz."

Typical boy, thought Polly, feeling annoyed. She should have guessed she'd have a hard time persuading her boyfriend through the doors of the de Young or the San Francisco Museum of Modern Art when there was a world-famous prison to look at instead.

The day had started with breakfast on the farmhouse veranda, looking out over the valley. They had eaten tofu scramble sautéed with loads of fresh veggies, garlic and paprika. Polly had volunteered to cook breakfast, and even though Ollie had looked a little suspicious at the mention of tofu, he had ended up eating three servings. "See, veggie food can be good if you actually season it," Polly had whispered to him as they took their empty plates into the kitchen. If the silence around the breakfast table had been anything to go by, Courtney and Willow still hadn't forgiven Polly's dad for taking Polly and Ollie to San Francisco for the day, but Polly was too relieved at the thought of the time that lay ahead of them – so free and sunny and full of promise – to care.

*

Swallowing her annoyance with Ollie, Polly sank back in her seat and gazed out the window. It had been a bit foggy driving from the airport earlier in the week, so she was waiting for an unobstructed view of the bay.

"You want to see Alcatraz, Ollie?" remarked Polly's dad after a while. "Take a look over there."

Ollie gave a whistle as he looked out of the car window. The great struts of the Golden Gate Bridge were looming before them, but his eyes were on the gleaming waters of the bay, and a small island topped with a ominous looking building. Alcatraz.

And suddenly they were on the bridge itself. Forgetting about art museums, Polly gazed up at the mighty red-orange span of the bridge. It was *enormous*. The two great towers seemed to soar off into the blue sky above them, and the twisted red cables striped the view from both sides of the car.

"No one ever escaped," Ollie was telling the window, still sounding awestruck as he stared at the famous prison island.

"Apart from Clint Eastwood," said Polly's dad. "Have you seen the movie *Escape from Alcatraz*?"

"Morris and the Anglin brothers didn't escape

alive," Ollie said at once. "I know the movie suggests that they did, but these Norwegian fishermen found a body. . ."

Her father and Ollie's voice faded out as Polly stared, mesmerized, at the bridge cables whipping past her window. The water beneath the bridge was said to be a hundred metres deep. A horrible thought had occurred to her and she was having trouble shaking it off. What if the whole bridge suddenly crashed into the sea below?

Thrum, thrum, thrum . . . went the wheels of the station wagon over the bridge surface.

"It's *possible* that the escapees swam to freedom," her dad was arguing with Ollie. "No one ever proved that body was Frank Morris."

"No way! The water out there is freezing, and choppy, and dangerous. They found an empty raft floating in the bay, didn't they? They drowned for sure!"

Ollie sounded positively ghoulish. Polly shivered. *Thrum, thrum, thrum* went the station wagon wheels. She fixed her eyes on the far side of the bridge. They would be fine. She was just being silly.

But the sense that the world might crumble at any moment beneath her feet stayed with her. Polly couldn't shift the sense of unease even as she, her dad and Ollie explored Golden Gate Park together, walked around the de Young Museum, and rode one of the iconic brown-and-cream cable cars up and over the hill and back down to the touristy Fisherman's Wharf. Now they were queuing for the boat ride out to Alcatraz. Polly still didn't feel right.

"Your dad said we'll go shopping after this," said Ollie, misreading Polly's silence as their boat cut through the deep blue water of the bay. "The Mission District park is on the way home. Alcatraz won't be so bad."

"Like the art museum wasn't so bad for you?" Polly's dad enquired, grinning at Ollie.

"You have a point," Ollie said, shooting an apologetic glance at Polly. "The park was nice, but the art kind of left me cold."

Polly's father looked amused. "They do say opposites attract."

Ollie laughed. Polly didn't. Being tourists had been a reminder her of how different she and Ollie were, and she didn't like it. *Mum and Dad were opposites,* she thought as the boat docked at the forbidding island prison. *And look how their relationship turned out.*

The tour of the prison was fascinating, but as they walked around Polly found that she was struggling to push down the feeling that something wasn't right. She didn't understand what was wrong with her, but she felt anxious and moody. Everywhere was so forbidding. The rusting wire, the machine-gun outposts, the great watchtower. Polly had to force herself to move out of the warm sunshine and into the cold and unforgiving prison building.

"Al Capone's cell!" Ollie exclaimed, pointing. "Pose there for me will you, Pols? Pretend you're a gangster. 'You talkin' to me?', that kind of thing. Go on!"

Polly stared at the bars, and the cramped space that had once held a human being. Her breathing felt wrong. She had to leave this place, right now, before something bad happened. She didn't know what. She just knew she had to leave, or she would fall into a dead faint on the cracked concrete floor. She backed away, her eyes darting for some kind of escape. Ollie's smile faltered.

"Sorry. . ." Polly pressed her hands to her chest.

Her heart was beating so fast she couldn't think. "I can't . . . I have to get out . . . please, let me out. . ."

She was running now, out into the sunlight again. Her breathing was all over the place. Her vision was beginning to darken as full-blown panic took hold. *Keep running. Don't trip or you'll fall off the rock and die in the sea like all the prisoners who tried to escape . . . drowned, or crushed against the rocks, or gunned down in the water. . .*

She was running upwards, because that was where the air was. That was how it felt to her, at least. She knew it made no sense but she had to get to the top where there would be nothing but clear air between her and the sky. . .

"Polly, come back!"

Her legs almost gave way beneath her as she reached the top, her lungs heaving and gasping and her whole body slick with a cold sweat. Gripping the railings, trying not to look down, Polly gazed at the shore – the towers of the city, the great Trans America pyramid. Everything seemed so serene, in such contrast to the turmoil in her heart and brain and body, and slowly she allowed herself to calm down.

Suddenly, all she felt was shame. What would Ollie and her dad think of her, running off like a lunatic in there? She'd always been a worrier, but this type of panic – this was new, and dark, and eating at her like a worm from the inside-out.

What was happening to her? Why couldn't she control herself?

TEN

"Polly!" Ollie was beside her now, heaving for breath with one hand pressed to his side. "What happened back there? What spooked you?"

Waves of embarrassment were crashing over Polly now, like the foaming water far below that was throwing itself at the rocks. "I'm sorry," she whispered. "I don't know what happened, I just . . . I had to get out."

"You're shivering!" Ollie exclaimed. He wrapped his arms around her and pulled her against him. "You scared me, running off like that."

Polly felt worse than ever. "I'm sorry," she repeated helplessly. Ollie's chest felt warm as she laid her cheek against the soft cotton of his shirt. Her stomach was still churning but she felt so much safer in Ollie's arms.

"At least we got a good view out of it," he joked, looking around at the vast stretch of water and mountains, the boats and the towers of the city and the red bridge arching over the bay. "I'd thank you for dragging me up here if I didn't have such a stitch in my side."

Polly didn't feel up to joking yet. She could hardly look at her boyfriend. *He must think I'm insane*, she thought unhappily. She'd behaved like a crazy person.

They both turned at the sound of puffing. Polly's father was leaning against the railings of the steps, red-faced and gasping.

"Whoo," he puffed. "I haven't run that fast up steps in a while. Is everything OK?"

"Polly got a fright," Ollie explained, hugging Polly a little tighter.

A fright, Polly thought dully. Ollie made it sound so simple, like she was a child who'd had a bad dream. *Then how come I'm still awake?* she wanted to say. How come a few kisses and cuddles hadn't taken the monsters away? She still felt – wrong. Broken, somehow. Like something wasn't fitting together inside her any more. Since they'd arrived in California, she'd wanted everything to be perfect. They only had a week here, so she had to take advantage of every minute. But nothing was going to plan. First there was Willow and Courtney and now she couldn't control her emotions. Waves of anxiety washed over her at the most unpredictable times and she didn't know how to stop it from happening.

"It's a pretty creepy place," Polly's dad said, nodding like he understood. "Prisoners frequently went insane, banged up for sixteen hours a day in those little cells."

"I'm fine," Polly blurted out, desperate to move the conversation on and forget any of this had happened. "I just felt a little claustrophobic, that's all. You guys continue with the tour if you want."

Her father checked his watch. "Next boat leaves in fifteen minutes," he said. "What do you say we try a little retail therapy to take the taste of this place away?"

Polly was only too glad to board the little white boat and sail back to shore. She smiled and posed at the railings as Ollie snapped pictures. She obediently lifted her hand on Ollie's instructions so he could take a snap of her 'holding' Alcatraz in her palm.

She answered her father's questions about where they should have dinner as if they were the most important questions in the world. And she felt separated from all of it, like she wasn't there at all. Like some part of her had stayed on Alcatraz behind bars, peering at the world from a distance.

I mustn't lose control like that again, was all she could think as they took the F-line streetcar from the Ferry Building to the vibrant Mission District. The thought made her worry about it even more. How would she know if another panic attack, if that's what it was, was coming? How could she avoid making a fool of herself again?

The Mission District took her mind off her feelings for a while. Holding Ollie's hand as they strolled along, Polly enjoyed the colourful murals that decorated the streets, the palm trees waving in the soft Californian wind, the unusual stores and the cheerful holiday crowd. There was a mariachi band playing somewhere, their brass instruments irresistibly jolly as they echoed around the area, and Polly found her feet tapping to the music whenever she paused outside a shop to gaze at the window displays.

You're going to be fine, she told herself a dozen times. *Focus on the good things and the bad things will go away.*

So she laughed at Ollie's cheesy jokes and enjoyed the way his eyes crinkled with affection whenever he looked at her, and slid her free hand through her father's arm whenever she could so that they could walk three abreast down the street.

"Do you want to go in there?" suggested Ollie, as Polly paused at a window display of beautiful original fashion that reminded her of her own style.

Polly found that she really did want to go inside. "Would you mind?" she said a little hesitantly. It was exactly the kind of shop that she loved, but it wasn't exactly boy-friendly.

"Ollie and I will get a coffee at that little kiosk across the road and he can tell me more about his soccer successes while we wait," her father said. "Take all the time you want."

The shop was cool, and smelled of jasmine. Polly studied the designs hanging from the rails artfully arranged around the shop, noting their unusual details: asymmetrical hemlines and layered fabrics, beautiful fastenings and bright patterns. There was nothing more soothing than the cool slip of silk between her fingers, or the comforting rub of soft cotton.

"I love your outfit. Where did you get it?"

Polly spun round, her fingers still grazing a soft mint green top with large buttons running down the back in a row. A gorgeously dressed assistant was smiling admiringly at her. Polly looked down at her vintage beach-umbrella print top and silver skirt with its red bow at the waistband.

"I made it," she said a little shyly.

The assistant's perfectly made-up eyes widened. "You *made* it? You are super-talented, it's *gorgeous*. Where did you find the fabric for the top? I would kill for fabric like that."

Polly had to laugh. She felt that way about fabric sometimes too. "In a charity shop in England."

The assistant sighed. "The English have such style."

"You're pretty stylish yourself," Polly had to point out.

The girl looked down at her sundress which had a repeating lemon-and-lime print. "Thanks," she said, looking pleased. "This dress is one of our bestsellers.

Let me know if I can help you with anything. Although I guess you know what you're looking for!"

Polly felt warm all over. She bought the top with the buttons and headed back into the street with an added bounce in her step. Her day had most definitely improved.

The shop assistant wasn't the only person to give her outfit a second glance on the streets of the Mission District. Two more girls stopped them, and asked Polly about her top.

"It's a British brand called Turned Around With Love," her father explained proudly, as Polly blushed with pleasure. "Very exclusive."

"Dad," Polly giggled as they made their way further along the street. "You make it sound like my designs are sold on Bond Street."

"Today, Paradise Farm and Heartside Bay Market," Ollie declared with a generous sweep of one arm, "tomorrow the world. I'm starving by the way. Where can we get something to eat?"

"It never takes long for you to get on to the subject of food," Polly teased.

The sun had started to dip over the two towers of

the Mission Dolores, San Francisco's oldest church in the heart of the Mission District. "There's a great Mexican place nearby," said Polly's dad. "Enchiladas like you wouldn't believe. My treat."

Polly felt more relaxed than she had all day as they sat outside in the setting sun, gazing out over the hills of the city with a mountain of smoky enchiladas between them. Courtney's dry quinoa felt a million miles away. She wished her life could be like this always. It was the perfect end to an oddly stressful day.

ELEVEN

If Courtney says the word "healthful" one more time, I won't be responsible for my actions, Polly thought a little grimly as she tied one of her hand-drawn heart-shaped price labels on to a hanger in the store barn the following day.

"Oh my," Courtney said, sucking her perfect teeth and studying the label on a packet of biscuits that Willow was setting out on the open wooden shelves by the till. "Have you seen how much sugar they put into these? Sugar is one of the great killers of our time. There are so many more healthful alternatives out there that people should be using. I swear by agave myself."

What in the world is agave? thought Polly idly. She

straightened the label so that it hung neatly down the front of the dress and picked up her pen to write the next one.

Willow grew bored with stacking biscuits and came to join Polly at her end of the barn. She leaned against the wall, fiddling with a long strand of hair. "Do you really think your stuff will sell in California?" she asked, eyeing a pair of overalls Polly had hemmed into shorts and painted with tiny white stars. "I don't mean to be rude, but you don't see many kids in my school wearing stuff like this."

Of course she meant to be rude. Otherwise, thought Polly, why say it? "I received several enquiries in San Francisco about the outfit I was wearing yesterday," she said as politely as she could. "Everyone seemed really interested in the idea of recycled fashion."

Willow studied the price label Polly had hung on the waistband of a black crepe skirt with row of gold studs around the waist. "You're asking a lot of money for this," she said, fingering the studs. "Were these from a hardware store or something?"

If Willow pulled any of the studs off the dress, Polly would take great pleasure in charging her the full price she was so doubtful about. "I think your mother needs you to help sort the tomatoes," she said, hoping Willow would take the hint.

Willow ignored that. "Don't you ever worry that people may have *died* in some of the stuff you recycle?" she said instead. "Don't you think that's kind of creepy?"

"Full-fat ice cream?" Courtney tutted, her hands on her hips as she peered into the large freezer by the doors. "Alex ought to stock natural sorbets. I know several healthful recipes that would be bestsellers for the farm."

"Ice cream is so bad for you," Willow agreed, running her hand along the delicate shell necklaces that Polly had arranged on a wide-branched, polished piece of driftwood, making them rattle.

More than anything, Polly longed to be out in the fields with Ollie and her dad. They had left after an early breakfast, discussing how the old red tractor had been converted to run on bio-fuel, ready to inspect the spelt crop higher up on the property and assess whether it was time to harvest or whether a few more days in the sun would fatten up the slim brown grains a little further. Polly had been happy enough with the plan at the time. She had so many plans for Turned Around With Love in the barn – the layout, the way she would group the colours – that she had almost run across the yard to get started. But from the moment Courtney and Willow had joined her in the store, everything started going downhill.

Her dad had taken her aside the previous evening, as they pulled into the darkening farmyard in the station wagon. "Give Courtney and Willow another chance, won't you Polly?" he pleaded. "OK, so Courtney can't cook and Willow doesn't have much in common with you, but it would mean so much to me if you would just try to get along. It's only for a week."

It was easy for Ollie, Polly thought sadly. Ollie rubbed along happily with everyone he ever met. But with Willow making snide cracks about her clothes and Courtney's obsession with "healthful" matters, she wasn't sure she would be able to stay polite for much longer. She was having enough trouble staving off the odd feelings of yesterday, fighting them back whenever they threatened to return. She still wasn't sure what had happened to her and she wished she could get rid of her uneasy feeling.

After a patchy night's sleep full of dreams of cramped prison cells and tumbling buildings, she had woken feeling tired and disjointed again. She felt threadbare, under-protected. It was hard to fight the feelings, and Willow and Courtney weren't helping.

"I'm bored," Willow announced. "Mom, can I Skype my friends?"

The moment Willow left the barn, Polly felt her mood lighten. She tweaked the necklaces on their driftwood display tree one more time, then stood back to admire the effect. Selling her clothing at the market stall had been one thing, but this was something else entirely. This was an actual *store*, with a curtained changing room and a carefully edited selection of clothes on the custom-made shelves and rails. Polly made a mental note to work on her website. If her designs took off in the States, it would be great to be able to sell them online.

"Well now," said Courtney, bustling over to where Polly was standing. "This is all looking very pretty. You have been working hard, haven't you?"

She's being nice, Polly reminded herself. *She's not*

talking about healthful anything. "Thank you," she said, feeling genuinely grateful. After Willow's string of hurtful remarks about her clothes, any praise at all felt like balm.

"Your father is such a kind person," said Courtney. "Letting you sell your fashions with us here on our little farm."

Polly tensed. Although she probably meant well, Courtney made it sound as if her father was doing her a favour. And what was with the "our"? *It's Dad's farm*, she wanted to shout. *Back off.*

"I'm sure you know how I feel about your father," Courtney continued warmly, taking Polly's hands in such a way that Polly felt screamingly awkward. "We may not have been together for long, but I know that our two souls were meant to come together in harmony on Paradise Farm."

Polly swallowed. She didn't feel up to any great confessions of the soul from Courtney. "That's great," she said weakly.

"I hope to marry Alex very soon," Courtney confided. "I know he wants more kids. We both want to fill this place with little children."

Polly's hands felt sweaty in Courtney's grip. Her

dad had told her it was early days. How come he and Courtney had talked about getting married and having kids already? She had lost so much of her father already. She'd lose even more of him if he had more children. She wanted desperately to stay in control, but this was too much information.

"I'm glad my dad's found someone to make him happy," she managed.

The anxiety was rising, like a sludgy brown tide. She felt it creeping through her body, clutching at her heart and lungs with sticky, murderous hands.

"I need some fresh air," she blurted, trying not to look as if she was wrenching herself away from Courtney's hands.

"Fresh air is so healthful," Courtney called after her as Polly stumbled as quickly as she could towards the doors. *Don't lose it*, she prayed, moving as fast as she could towards the house. *Stay in control. Stay in. . .*

She faltered as she rounded the corner of the barn. Willow and Ollie were standing together, laughing about something near the chicken pen. Willow had slipped her arms around Ollie's waist, her head tipped back and her hair pouring like golden silk down her back, laughing as Ollie looked into her eyes. . .

A tide of panic crashed over her, drowning her.

TWELVE

Polly whirled around and ran towards the farmhouse. Her heartbeat had accelerated, clunking and banging in her chest like it was about to burst free of her rib cage. If felt like she was having a heart attack. Her legs . . . her whole body was shaking so badly that she could barely coordinate her fingers to turn the door handle.

I'm dying, was all she could think as she ran into the cool hallway, reaching desperately for the stair rail. *I'm having a heart attack.*

If she was dying, why was she running away from the people who might be able to help her? Why was she taking the stairs two at a time on hopelessly trembling legs, her sweaty hands slipping on the polished wooden stair rail? She couldn't *think*. Her chest felt like it was in a vice, and someone was turning the screws tighter and tighter.

Polly reached the landing and dropped to all fours. She was having trouble breathing. *Not far now*, she thought dimly. Her chest hurt. *Not far to my room. Everything will be OK when I reach my room.* Her mouth felt dry, her fingers and toes felt numb. *Bang bang bang* went her heart.

Reaching her room after what felt like for ever, she shut the door and slid to the ground, burying her hot face in her shaking hands. Her body felt like it was going into shutdown. It was the most frightening thing she had ever experienced.

Breathe. Breathe. Breathe.

Polly sat there, slumped on the rag rug on the polished wooden floor, fear and terror in every part of her. She couldn't have moved, even if her body had let her.

After what felt like a lifetime, the trembling slowed and stopped. Her dress was soaked with sweat and clung to her hot body. The sense of nausea was ebbing. Polly got unsteadily to her feet and went to the toilet to splash water on her face. Then she lay down on the floor of the bathroom, curled up in a ball, the cool tiles pressing against her hot cheek.

She was losing her dad to his new California family.

She was losing Ollie to Willow.

She was losing her mind.

And she felt powerless to control any of it.

My world is breaking apart, she thought.

The bathroom floor was comforting. She felt the imprint of the tiles on her skin. But dimly she knew she couldn't lie there for ever. Her legs felt as unsteady as a newborn lamb's as she stood up. Her breathing was back to a more normal level. The worries were still there, but the awful panic, the terrible chest pains had faded away.

Polly took off her soaked dress and took a long shower, turning her face to the sharp needles of water. She felt weary as she towelled herself dry and pulled on leggings and a tank top. Then she lay unseeingly on her bed and stared at the bedroom door.

She couldn't go downstairs. What if she had another attack? Darkness began to fill her again and she started to cry. On top of the whole business with her dad, and

Courtney, and Ollie, and Willow, she realized she was feeling anxious about feeling anxious. It felt like a horrible trap.

She didn't know how long she lay there for. She simply watched the sunlight tracking its way across the bedroom floor, marking the time floorboard by floorboard.

Someone knocked. Polly hid her face in her duvet as Ollie put his head around the door.

"There you are!" he said. "Can I come in?" He registered her hidden face. "What's the matter?"

The image of Ollie and Willow in the yard together flashed into Polly's mind. Polly shook her head silently. What was she supposed to say? Ollie crossed the room and sat beside her.

"Hey, talk to me, Pols," he said.

Polly shook her head again. She didn't want to know what had happened with Willow. She didn't think she could take the embarrassment of Ollie telling her he had fallen for her. And if she talked about her Dad and Courtney getting married, she might get that awful feeling in her chest again, and be unable to breathe for good this time.

"Something's happened," Ollie pressed her. "Have you hurt yourself? Did Courtney say something?"

"Dad and Courtney are getting married." It was all Polly could choke out.

Ollie looked shocked. "They are? He didn't say anything to me in the field today. When did this happen? Are you sure?"

"Courtney told me in the barn this morning."

Ollie made a face. "You don't want to believe too much of what Courtney tells you. That woman likes quinoa too much to be completely sane."

Polly smiled weakly at his joke. "They want to have more children."

Ollie put his arms round her. "Well, if they do, that's nice isn't it? You would have brothers and sisters."

She didn't want brothers and sisters. She wanted to go home, to Heartside Bay, where Ollie was still hers and everything was *normal* again. Or as normal as her life ever got. She thought of Ollie and Willow together in the yard again, laughing together. Beautiful, blonde, confident. The perfect couple. Her stomach clenched. No boy could resist someone as pretty as Willow.

"I would understand, you know," she said as

bravely as she could, looking into Ollie's familiar blue eyes. "If you wanted to go out with Willow instead of me. At least, I would try to understand. If it made you happy, I would."

Ollie looked confused. "What are you talking about? I don't want to go out with Willow."

"But I'd understand if you *did* want to go out with her," Polly whispered. "She's so perfect. Not like me. I'm such a mess."

"You're not a mess. You're lovely. How many times do I have to tell you before you believe me? I love you, Polly. Only you."

In her present state, Polly couldn't even enjoy those magical words. "I saw you in the yard with her," she said, steeling herself for the guilt she feared she would see in his eyes. "You had your arms around her."

"*She* had her arms around *me*," he corrected. "I thought we'd dealt with this already? Willow's an annoying flirt."

Polly so wanted to feel reassured by his words. "So you don't like her?" she asked. She felt so pathetic, asking, but she had to be *sure*.

"I'm being nice to her for your sake, Polly," he said.

"For your dad's sake. When will you believe how much you mean to me?"

Was that annoyance Polly could hear in her boyfriend's voice? *He's getting tired of me*, she thought. *How much more of my crazy behaviour and endless insecurity is he going to put up with? How much longer can I go on feeling like this?* They were questions she didn't feel up to answering.

THIRTEEN

Two more days, Polly thought. *Only two more.*

Despite everything, Polly didn't want her time in California to end. She loved it here. But she was so *tired* of the emotional mess inside her head. She had wanted the trip be perfect, and it hadn't been. She couldn't suppress the worried thoughts that ran through her mind at unpredictable times. She couldn't just be happy. It seemed so easy for Ollie, and she felt ashamed of the way she kept freaking out in front of him. She knew he loved her, so why couldn't she silence those niggling doubts that ran through her head about him and Willow? Courtney and Willow hadn't grown any easier to like over the past couple of days, and when she thought about leaving her dad with them on Sunday, she grew even more anxious. All she could think about was that he might have married Courtney by the next time she came to visit. She might never have him to herself again.

Reaching into her beach bag, she slapped on a fresh layer of suncream and adjusted the sunglasses on her nose. She pulled her hat a little more firmly on to her head and twitched her towel so that it lay straight on the fine sand. Then she tried to focus on the view in front of her and ignore the worries inside her head.

The beach was every bit as incredible as her father had promised. Wild, and long, the waves of the Pacific curling and crashing away into the distance in both directions. Polly could feel the weight of the world's biggest ocean in every shock of water as it struck the sand. The smashing, curling foam made the surf back home in Heartside Bay seem very feeble in comparison.

The great golden expanse was backed by a long line of sand dunes all tufted with marram grass and speckled with tiny flowers. There was no one here but them: her, Ollie, her dad, Courtney and Willow. She wished Lila, Rhi and Eve were here too – they would love it.

Trying to get more comfortable, Polly adjusted her bikini: a thinly striped black-and-white two-piece with high-waisted bottoms. Back at home she felt very chic wearing it. Very Audrey Hepburn. But Willow's judgemental face as Polly took off her beach cover-up had made her felt embarrassed that she wasn't wearing something more modern.

Shouts of laughter wafted up the beach towards her towel from the water's edge. Courtney and Willow, looking near identical in the tiniest of string bikinis – Courtney in yellow, Willow in pink. Their long limbs perfectly tanned, their hair slicked with protective sun oil, their bodies gleaming with health and sunshine, they were running and shrieking in the surf. Her father, in surf shorts, was chasing them through the surf with Ollie hot on his heels. They were bending down and flicking the water upwards, soaking the girls amid shouts of laughter.

Ollie's skin had tanned to a wonderful rich bronze, and his hair – as Polly had predicted – had turned almost white in just a week. With a scattering of freckles on his fine straight nose and his teeth a blinding white flash in his brown face, he was the perfect model of Californian health. His head seemed to turn more and more often towards Willow's body. Even from this distance, Polly could sense that he was trying not to gawk. She couldn't blame him. The Californian girl's body was utterly perfect. In her heart, Polly knew that she shouldn't care about looks. She was a feminist after all. It was her brain that mattered, not her body. And normally she didn't mind being short and small – it was easier to fit into a lot of vintage clothing that way. But she felt so childlike when she stood next to the tall, curvy Willow. She glanced down despondently at her flat chest and sighed.

Polly scratched miserably at a large red mosquito bite that had mysteriously appeared at the top of her pale thigh. She wished she hadn't come to the beach. She felt like a gatecrasher at a party. Five was a hopeless number, especially when the other four matched each other so well.

Seeing her looking, Ollie waved. For a moment, Polly's stomach dissolved with love.

"I'm starving," he grinned, jogging towards her with his white-blond hair flopping into his eyes. "I hope there's something edible in that picnic basket."

Polly and her dad had spent ages packing the basket with gorgeous organic goodies from the farm that morning. There were fat tomatoes, juicy cucumbers, peaches and nectarines and grapes. There were brown rolls filled with mozzarella and fresh basil, asparagus quiche and bottles of natural lemonade. At the bottom of the basket were pitta and hummus, tortilla chips and fresh salsa, cornbread and crunchy little radishes. Polly unpacked it all carefully.

"Nothing beats a sandy sandwich," said her father as they all sprawled around the checked picnic blanket beneath the large white sunshade Courtney had packed.

"Sand is great for the digestion," said Ollie with a solemn look on his face.

"Don't be silly, Ollie," said Courtney, a little disapprovingly.

"We don't know where the sand has been," said Willow, wrinkling her perfect brown nose.

"I bet it's travelled a thousand miles," said Polly's father, examining his sandy forearm. The mica in the sand caught the sun, glittering a hundred times over.

"Rolled over and over in the surf for a million years until it is ground to pure powder. You can't get much more organic that this."

Ollie turned his laugh into a cough at the annoyed look on Courtney's face. Polly wanted to laugh as well, but she couldn't seem to make her mouth turn up at the edges.

"Who wants to play beach volleyball?" suggested Willow, jumping up from the blanket the moment the last fat grapes had been pulled from their stems. "I brought a ball."

Courtney clapped girlishly. "I love beach volleyball! Count me in."

"You don't mind if I play, do you?" Ollie asked hopefully as Polly's dad and Courtney drew some markings in the sand and Willow fetched a ball from the depths of her bright silver beach bag.

"Of course not," Polly said automatically. *One, two, three, four*, she thought: her dad, Ollie, Courtney and Willow. Two on each side of the net. Polly the odd one out, once again.

"Why don't you join in?" Ollie asked. He extended a hand towards her.

The last thing Polly wanted to do was leap around in front of Courtney and Willow. "Five's a difficult number," she hedged. "Playing with four is much better. I'll watch."

She felt like she'd done a lot of watching today.

Her dad and Courtney took one side of the marked-out volleyball court. Ollie and Willow took the other. Courtney and Willow both hit the ball smoothly and stylishly, stretching out their bodies for the more difficult balls, rolling in the sand with squeals of laughter whenever they over-reached themselves. Polly's dad had a mean volleyball serve, smashing the ball in Ollie's direction. Although Ollie had the least experience in the game from the looks of things, he gave as good as he got.

It was impossible not to feel jealous as Polly watched Ollie and Willow working as a team, thumping the ball perfectly every time, and hugging each other in celebration with every point scored.

No matter how many times she reminded herself of how much Ollie loved her, and all the things he'd said about Willow being an annoying flirt, she couldn't help watching the two of them together and wondering. She also noticed her dad was being particularly attentive to Courtney and Willow. There were endless compliments, and kisses, and hugs. She knew he was trying to make it up to them both for the day he'd spent with just her and Ollie, but it was still hard to watch. It really did look as if he loved her, as if he wanted to marry her and start a whole new family to go with his whole new life.

I might as well be invisible, she thought sadly.

Ollie and Willow won the game by two points. With much whooping, they both ran down to the ocean to leap in and cool down among the waves as Courtney started packing up the picnic. Their slick blond heads bobbed together in the glittering water like two beautiful seals.

"There's a great view on that dune up there," said Polly's dad, nodding towards a high dune with a nodding head of tall grasses. "Let's take a walk, Pollydolly."

Polly felt grateful for her father's interest. She pulled at the straps of her bikini in a bit to make them lie a little straighter on her shoulders and followed him across the hot sand.

"I haven't asked about what happened at Alcatraz,"

he said as they reached the top of the dune, looking sideways at her. "I was hoping you might tell me of your own accord."

The panic of that day gripped Polly around the throat again. "It was nothing. I was just being stupid," she said.

He was looking intently at her. "Have you had a panic attack before?"

A panic attack. So that's what it was. Polly thought about the awful attack she'd experienced after seeing Ollie and Willow together. The crushing pain in her chest, the sweat soaking her to the skin. "Hardly ever," she lied.

Part of her wanted her dad to keep pressing her. It was scary and lonely, feeling the way she did. The rest of her hoped he wouldn't. He already thought she was crazy enough.

"I want to help, Polly," he said.

How? Polly thought wearily. *This is something I have to deal with by myself.* "Alcatraz was a weird one-off, Dad. Honestly. It's probably part of the jet lag. It's all been a bit weird, coming back to California. Meeting your new family."

"If you're sure?"

Polly wrapped her arms around her dad's warm waist and hugged him hard. "I'm sure," she said.

I'm not going crazy. I can't be.

FOURTEEN

The air was filled with the sound of rushing planes. Landing, taxiing, taking off. Wings banked, landing gears grinded. The air shimmered with heat and the familiar smell of plane fuel.

Polly was relieved that Courtney and Willow hadn't come to the airport, reserving their goodbyes in the farmyard instead. Even Courtney couldn't object to Polly saying goodbye to her father by herself.

"It's been wonderful to meet you," she said, embracing Polly gingerly. "You must come back and visit us really soon."

"Really soon," Willow echoed, her eyes firmly on Ollie.

And then the bags were in the boot and the station

wagon was trundling down the winding driveway, the farm's fattest brown cow watching as they passed. Polly stared out of the rear window for as long as the wind turbine was visible. Then she turned round and clasped Ollie's hand tightly and thought about Heartside Bay waiting for them on the far side of the Atlantic Ocean.

"Last call," said her dad now, checking his watch as they stood on the bustling airport concourse. "You kids OK finding the gate?"

Polly threw her arms around him. "I'm going to miss you so much, Dad," she said desperately. *And you probably won't miss me at all.*

She felt so torn. She wanted him to be happy, but she wanted him for herself. She wished he was still with her mum, but she knew he was happier here with Courtney. She longed for so many things that all seemed to contradict each other.

Ollie shook her father's hand. "Great to meet you, Alex. Thank you so much, I've had an amazing time."

"We've loved having you. Both of you." Her father hugged Polly one more time. She clung to him like a rock in a stormy sea. "You have to go now or you'll miss the flight," he said, gently disentangling her arms from around his neck. "Call me as soon as you get home, OK?"

Polly felt numb as they walked away, through the check-in gates, past security and into the departures lounge. Ollie kept his arm firmly around her, knowing how she was feeling perhaps, and kissing her head.

"What a trip," he said, grinning at Polly as they boarded. "We'll have so much to tell everyone, won't we?"

Polly was concentrating too hard on not crying to answer. Luckily Ollie didn't notice.

Polly had a window seat again for the trip home. As the plane roared down the runway and into the blue Californian sky, Polly flattened her forehead to the window and thought about her father, way down there, already a tiny speck of nothing and growing smaller all the time. Further away from her than ever. Her eyes blurred and the tears finally began to fall.

The sky was a solid grey as the plane touched down the following morning. Stiff and exhausted from too little sleep in an upright position, Polly could hardly keep her eyes open as they unloaded their hand luggage from the overhead racks, queued for customs and waited endlessly for their bags to emerge from the carousel. She texted her mum to say they'd arrived. Her dad too. It was easier than the thought of talking to him. What if Courtney answered the phone? Besides, it was gone midnight in San Francisco. She didn't want to wake him up.

The train home seemed to take for ever. She laid her head on Ollie's lap and fell asleep with his hand stroking her hair. The next thing she knew, he was gently shaking her awake.

"Wake up, sleepyhead," he whispered. "We're home."

Polly sat up, disoriented. If anything, her nap on the train had made her feel groggier. Rubbing her eyes, she stared out of the window at the familiar station, hearing the sounds of whistles blowing and the familiar day-to-day sounds of the town in the background. It was familiar but strange at the same time. At least here there wouldn't be any unpleasant surprises waiting for her.

"Taxi," Ollie suggested as they staggered out of the station with their bags. "You look dead on your feet."

Polly nodded gratefully, and let Ollie do all the talking as the bags were loaded into the back of a blue taxi cab.

"Where've you been, mate?" asked the taxi driver. "Somewhere sunny by the looks of it."

"California."

"All right for some."

"Looking forward to seeing your mum?" Ollie asked as the taxi pulled into the traffic.

Polly was mainly looking forward to collapsing in her bed and sleeping for the next century. She simply smiled, and let Ollie rabbit on about San Francisco, and the chickens, and the tractor, and the spiced quinoa ("Never again!"). And then they were outside his house and he was kissing her goodbye and promising to call her later and unloading his bags and waving. Polly rested her head against the car seat and resisted the urge to close her eyes as the cab took her home.

A removals van was standing outside her house.

Large men in blue overalls were carrying boxes back and forth. Polly stared in exhausted confusion. What had happened? Who was moving out?

"Seven pound fifty, love," the cabbie said.

Polly handed over the money without taking her eyes off the van. The familiar fear was gripping at her insides, her mind rushing through a thousand different reasons for there being a removals van outside her house, all of them bad. Her mum was leaving. She had lost her job. They had been evicted from their home—

"Polly!"

Her mother came running out of the house, arms extended in welcome. Polly let herself be embraced. She realized boxes were being taken *into* the house, not out.

"Honey, you got back so early!" her mother enthused, kissing her. "You look tired, come inside. Was it a good flight?"

"What's happening?" Polly managed to ask.

Her mother pulled her into the house. "Surprise!" she said in excitement. "Beth is moving in with us. Isn't that fantastic? We wanted to have everything done by the time you arrived, but the moving company lost half of Beth's boxes so they're just bringing them in now. We've been painting too. You should have seen this place three days ago. Chaos!"

"It's still chaos, Gin," laughed Beth Andrews, her mum's partner, from the kitchen door. Her hair was pulled back into a messy ponytail and there was a smudge of primrose-yellow paint on her cheek. "Welcome home, sweetheart," she said, hugging Polly tightly. She waved her yellow paintbrush under Polly's nose. "What do you think of the colour? Your mother wanted orange but I said that would be too strong."

"And of course, Beth is right," said Polly's mother, going up to her partner and giving her a warm kiss. "She has a far better eye for colours than me. I would have had this place looking like a Jaffa orange, given half a chance."

"What do you think?" Beth prompted.

The two women gazed expectantly at Polly. Two men in overalls staggered past, carrying a large armchair past Polly and into the living room. Polly realized belatedly that room had changed colour too, from cream to a pale purple.

"It's great," she heard herself say, from somewhere very far away.

She stared at the unfamiliar furniture, the boxes of books and knick-knacks littering the hallway. Her home didn't feel like her home any more. It wasn't great at all. It was all wrong.

FIFTEEN

"I knew you'd like it!" said her mother happily. "We'll help you in with your bags. You have to tell us all about your trip, we can't wait to hear what a fantastic time you've had!"

Polly watched as her mother and Beth gave each other an affectionate hug. She couldn't even find the energy to smile at how cute they were. Her legs felt like lead as she climbed the stairs, her mother and Beth pulling her suitcases up behind them.

"Tea?" said her mother brightly as Polly sat down on her bed and stared at her hands.

"I'm pretty tired," Polly replied quietly. "I think I'll have a little nap."

The way she was feeling, she wished she could sleep for ever.

"Leave her be, Gin," she heard Beth say. "She looks exhausted. That red-eye flight is a killer. Your body will be out of sync for a few days, Polly. Take it easy, OK?"

Her mother fussed around her, asking again if she needed a drink, a shower – anything. Polly shook her head over and over. She just wanted to be alone. It was a blessed relief when the bedroom door closed and she was left by herself.

Ollie would be calling at any moment. Polly switched her phone off and slid it inside the drawer in her bedside table. Unable even to find the energy to take her travel-stained clothes off, she tipped sideways until her cheek met the cool cotton of her pillow. She lay like that, unmoving. Hardly even thinking. Compared to the maelstrom of the past week, her mind felt oddly still. She just lay quietly, eyes closed, her knees pulled into her body, making herself as small and safe as she could.

When she opened her eyes again, her body felt stiff and the muscles in her legs were screaming. She must have slept. She had no idea how long for. She unfolded herself gently, sat up and stared at her curtains. They hadn't been drawn but it was dark out. It felt late.

She couldn't work out how she was feeling. Was she hungry? The thought of food turned her stomach. The thought of talking to her mum and Beth turned it even more. Quietly she tiptoed down the stairs, helped herself to an apple, and tiptoed back again.

Her bed looked more inviting than ever. This time, she managed to take off her clothes and slip on some pyjamas. There was nothing on TV. She had no energy for reading. She lay down and went back to sleep again, and dreamed of darkness and shaking mountains that rained down boulders as big as houses.

Somehow it was morning. Where was the time going? Was it Tuesday? Wednesday? Polly wasn't sure. At some point in the night she had gone downstairs again, finding a banana and a bread roll and a glass of water. The banana skin lay accusingly on her duvet cover, brown and curling. It made Polly wonder if she was somehow sleeping her life away, like Rip van Winkle in the fairy tale. Opening her bedside drawer, she withdrew her phone and switched it on. Three missed calls and a text message from Ollie.

Asleep? Academy training starts 2moro, will call after xx

It was already tomorrow, she realized. Ollie would be coaching at the summer school all day.

She found the energy from somewhere to unpack. Most of her clothes had been washed at the farm, and smelled faintly of Californian detergent. Polly buried her nose in the folds of fabric, and inhaled, and pictured her father standing beside her. Then she hung the clothes neatly in her wardrobe, draped the top from the store in the Mission over the end of her bed, closed up her suitcase and set it down beside the door so that it aligned perfectly with the doorframe.

She suddenly felt a deep yearning to see her girlfriends: Lila, Eve, Rhi. Someone she could be herself with. Someone she could talk to without pretending that everything was fine.

When she dialled Rhi, all she got was an unavailable dial tone. Polly knew Rhi was going on holiday with her dad sometime in August. It looked like she had gone, and to somewhere with no signal. Eve's number went straight to voicemail. She was working. After Christmas, the summer was the busiest time for party-planning, which Eve did part-time.

She called Lila. Lila's parents were always too busy for holidays. Her mother was a psychotherapist and couldn't leave her private practice. As for her dad, it was an unwritten rule that police chiefs never took holidays. The chances of catching Lila were better than the other two.

But there was no answer on Lila's mobile. The answerphone on her landline clicked in after three rings. Lila's mother's voice floated into Polly's ear, her voice tone and encouraging. The perfect voice for a therapist.

"I'm sorry no one can take your call. Please leave a message. If it is urgent, please call. . ." An 0800 number followed.

Polly hung up. She stood holding her phone limply in her hand, gazing unseeingly out of the window for a while, her phone in her hand. The sky was grey, just as it had been the day she had returned from the States.

Maybe no days had passed at all since her return. Maybe time had stopped all together. She couldn't decide what to do. She couldn't decide anything. No Rhi, no Eve, no Lila. Ollie would be kicking balls around for enthusiastic kids desperate to blow off steam in the long and boring summer holiday. She couldn't reach him either.

Polly got back into bed and drew the covers over her head. She slept again.

Day faded to night, and back to day. The smell of paint and turpentine wafted through the cracks in the door as Beth and her mother's decorating progressed, but in Polly's room everything remained much the same. She had a faint memory of Beth putting her head around the bedroom door, offering tea and food. Cups littered her bedside table, and plates of uneaten sandwiches and fruit queued up by her bed. She didn't want any of it.

"It'll be the jet lag, Polly love. You'll be right as rain tomorrow." She thought it had been her mother who had said that, but it might just as easily have been Beth. If this was jet lag, Polly wasn't sure she felt up to flying long-haul ever again.

When she wasn't sleeping, Polly tortured herself with visions of her friends and family living their lives without her.

Her father would be relieved that she had left. *Polly's a strange little thing*, she imagined him saying to Courtney on their wind-blown Pacific beach. *But too much like her mother for me. . .*

Whatever are we going to do with her funny clothes? Courtney would reply. *No one's buying them. They're taking up room in the store. We should find something else to sell instead.*

Ollie and Willow had probably been kissing in the hay barn when she wasn't looking. Laughing together about how blind Polly was. How odd, how uninteresting.

You're the one for me, Willow. I'm only with Polly out of pity. She's so fragile. . . But I'm so bored with her neediness.

What did Ollie ever see in me? Polly thought wearily. *He's better off without me.*

Her phone rang intermittently. Polly ignored it, until it ran out of charge and stopped ringing all together. She couldn't seem to snap out of this deep, dark sense of being at the bottom of a well, looking up at a tiny circle of sky and life and air way above her head. The world was functioning without her.

The depth of her misery frightened Polly. She'd never felt like this before, even on her worst days. She didn't want anyone to see her like this. Nobody at all.

SIXTEEN

"I think you've had enough sleep now, Polly," said Polly's mother, coming into Polly's bedroom on Thursday morning. She picked up the half-dead bananas and the crusted sandwiches between two fingers and dropped them in the bin. "Things to do, places to go. Come on, up you get."

Polly's eyes were gummed with sleep. Her hair felt stiff and unwashed, her sheets damp with perspiration. She shielded her gaze as her mother opened the curtains to let the light in. "Go away, Mum," she croaked.

Her mother was opening the windows, wafting her hands vigorously from side to side. "Urgh, it's so stale and frowsty in here," she complained. "How many cups of undrunk tea do you have in this room? No wonder Beth and I are having trouble finding enough mugs for coffee."

The top of the well was a long, long way above Polly's head. Her mother couldn't see her. Couldn't hear her. She felt as if she was shouting, trying to make her voice float up the deep black shaft and out into the light. "It's fine. Leave it, Mum. I'll do it."

Her mother had picked up Polly's phone now and was frowning at its blank screen. "You haven't plugged in your phone, Polly! It's dead as a dodo. I'll plug it in for you, shall I? There should be enough hot water for a shower if you hurry."

"I don't want a shower. I don't want anything."

A crease of concern appeared between her mother's brows. "Ollie's called us several times today already, asking about you. Have you spoken to him since you got back?"

Polly buried her head under her pillow again. "Go away," she mumbled again.

Her mother finally seemed to hear her. "I expect to hear the shower in ten minutes, Polly, or I'll be back. And don't think I won't tear the duvet off you because I will."

Polly made herself get out of bed. She took a shower as instructed, but could hardly feel the water. *I am not here,* she thought. *I am nothing.* She felt as insubstantial as her ghostly reflection in the plane window.

Polly made her way slowly downstairs, and sat quietly at the table, and stared at the pile of toast that Beth put under her nose. She could sense her mother and Beth exchanging glances over her head. Her mother sat opposite her, and reached for her hands.

"What's the matter, love? Are you missing your dad?"

Even shaking her head was an effort today.

"I'm sure he's missing you," her mother said. She meant it kindly, Polly knew. "There's still plenty of summer holiday left. Are you running the market stall this weekend?"

Polly hadn't given the market stall a moment's thought since her return. She shook her head once more.

"Why not?"

A fresh vision arose in Polly's mind of the designs she'd left behind in California, bundled into a corner of her dad's barn and forgotten. She shrugged. "No stock," she said.

Because her mum and Beth were watching her, she pasted a smile on her face and ate the toast and answered their questions in as few words as possible. Then she went back up to her room and shut the door and lay down and stared at the ceiling.

Her charged phone rang.

"There you are!" Ollie exclaimed when Polly plucked up the courage to pick up. "I've been calling and calling!"

"My phone was dead," Polly said. "Sorry."

"You sound strange, Pols. What's up?"

I'm losing my mind. "How's the academy?" she managed to ask.

"Fun. The kids are adorable. Some of them are pretty talented too. Listen, I don't have long – I'm on my lunch. You want to meet up later?"

"I'm still pretty tired," Polly whispered. If she saw him, she'd lose her resolve to let him go.

She could hear the hurt in his voice. "Oh. Right. Well, let's do it another night then. I'll call you later, OK?"

Polly unplugged her phone again as soon as he had hung up. She put it in her drawer, deep beneath her clothes. She wanted so badly to phone him back, beg and plead with him to help her. But what could he do? What could anyone do? She couldn't even explain what was happening to her, so how could anyone help?

Her mother came in without knocking. "Polly love, can I talk to you?" She took Polly's silence for consent, and sat at the bottom of her bed.

"What do you want to talk about?"

"I know it must seem strange, being back here after your week with your dad," her mother began. "I expect you found it difficult, being back in San Francisco."

You have no idea, Polly thought.

"But you had a good time, didn't you?" her mother went on anxiously. "Your dad phoned me yesterday, full of all the things you got up to."

I bet he didn't tell you about Courtney though.

"He said your designs are flying out of his store. You've made a real success of your market stall. You have a lovely boyfriend. You have plenty of summer work with Mr Gupta, waitressing at all the upcoming summer weddings. You're doing so well, Polly. I'm so proud of who you are becoming."

Polly wanted to weep. Her mother was trying to show her all the good things she had in her life, and everything her mum was saying was true. She did have a successful stall, and Ollie was everything she'd ever wanted in a boyfriend. So what was the matter with her? Why couldn't she feel happy about anything any more?

Polly spent most of Friday sitting at her desk and gazing out of the window. If she looked hard enough, she could see the glitter of the sea. The beach would be full of day-trippers, and the air would smell of chips and suncream. She wondered about her friends, what they were all doing. She felt lonelier than ever, watching the sun as it tracked across the sky towards the cliffs.

"What is it, Mum?" she sighed, turning round at the telltale creak of her bedroom door.

Ollie was standing in the doorway, frowning at her. "Hi," he said after a moment. He raised his hands, jazz-style. "It's the weekend!"

Like the weekend mattered, Polly thought.

"Your mum and Beth thought it would be nice to go to the beach for a picnic this evening," he said, scooping her out of her chair for a kiss. "Beth said she'd do a barbecue. And guess what? Rhi and Eve are going to be there!"

Polly felt a brief flicker of interest. "I thought they were away? They didn't pick up when I called them."

"Eve was working for the first part of the week. Rhi's around. What do you say?"

"I told you on the phone, I'm still very tired," Polly began.

Ollie steamrollered over her. "You'll perk up when we get down there. Rhi and Eve are desperate to hear about California. I said we'd be there at six, OK? I have to run a couple of errands first, but I'll come back and pick you up in an hour."

He wouldn't take no for an answer. Polly found herself gazing into her wardrobe as the front door slammed. She couldn't see anything she wanted to wear. Her hair hung in dull strands around her face. Her eyes looked too big for her pale face. How was she supposed to get ready for a party looking like this?

She spent a long time on her make-up, only to wash it off again. Dresses were tried on and discarded. Tops too, and trousers. Soon her room was awash with fabric in piled heaps all over the carpet. She could feel the first flicker of a headache.

Snap out of it, she told herself, with a sudden flush of resolve. *These are your friends. They won't care if you wear a bin bag.*

She pulled a plain black dress from the back of her closet. It would have to do. She couldn't be bothered to try on anything else. Polly brushed her hair and shook her head back and forth, trying to kick start some kind of feeling. Anything would be better than this dullness that had invaded her. But she just felt bland and exhausted. She sat perfectly still, the brush still in her hand.

I want to see my friends, she thought tearfully. *I need them. But I can't do this.*

The clock downstairs chimed six o'clock. Polly stared at her brush. There was a gentle knock on the door.

"You ready?" said Ollie.

Polly could see her mother hovering in the

corridor behind her boyfriend. *They're in this together*, she thought, and she suddenly felt furious at her helplessness and misery. And so she threw her hairbrush at Ollie.

He leaped back, startled as the brush clattered against the doorframe. "Poll, what—"

"Leave me alone!" Polly screamed, with every scrap of feeling she still had left. "I wish everyone would just *leave me alone*!"

SEVENTEEN

It took Polly half an hour to convince her mother and Ollie that she was fine, she was just having trouble throwing off her jet lag.

"It was very nice of Beth to offer to do a barbecue," she said, feeling hot with embarrassment, once everyone had calmed down and her hairbrush had been restored to its proper place and she'd finished crying on Ollie's shoulder as he soothed her and brought her back to earth. "I'm sorry I'm not being much fun at the moment."

"It doesn't matter," her mother said, stroking her shoulder. "We can do it another day. You mustn't worry about it."

Polly swallowed the tears that constantly threatened

to swamp her and nodded. *You mustn't worry.* How she longed not to worry.

Ollie hugged her a little tighter as Polly's mother quietly left the room. "Good job you've got such a bad aim," he joked, softly stroking her hair. "You could have taken my eye out."

She felt worse than ever. "I'm so sorry. Everything just got . . . too much. I'm fine now," she added quickly.

"You don't look fine."

Polly wondered if he was comparing her to Willow. Tall, tanned, happy Willow. "No one ever warns you how long it takes to sort out your body clock," she said feebly.

Ollie was still looking at her with what looked horribly like pity in his eyes. She wished he would stop looking at her. His eyes were so blue, they almost hurt.

"I really am very tired," she said pleadingly.

He rubbed his hands through his hair. "Fine," he said, almost to himself. "Get some sleep. We'll talk in the morning. Before the wedding, OK?"

Polly thought of her dad and Courtney. *They* were getting married. The thought hollowed her out all over again.

"You remember the wedding?" Ollie prompted. "You, waitressing for Mr Gupta? Noon tomorrow? You have remembered, haven't you?"

Polly had a faint memory that she was supposed to be waitressing at a themed wedding for wedding manager Mr Gupta the following day. She had no idea where it was, or whether there was a dress code. She'd dressed up as all kinds of things for Mr Gupta's weddings: vampires, angels, goths and fairies. What was this one? She racked her brains for details, but nothing was coming up.

"Of course I remember," she said. "We'll talk tomorrow. Yes. Tomorrow."

When Ollie had gone, Polly lay back on her bed and stared once more at her ceiling. If she couldn't even get out of the door to see her friends at the beach, how was she supposed to do the wedding for a hundred people she didn't know? How could she walk around a strange room with a smile on her face and a tray in her hands when her whole world had ground to a halt?

Polly didn't call Mr Gupta on Saturday morning. He wouldn't notice she was missing. No one would, and if they did she'd pretend she'd forgotten. The other waitresses would cope fine without her. The whole *world* was getting along just fine, without her playing any part at all. She spent the morning looking idly through her clothes she had pulled out the day before, wondering if she should donate them all to charity. The bright colours and patterns which she normally loved seemed garish and unbearable. She was ignoring her phone, which seemed to buzz every five minutes. The repetitive action soothed the dull thump in her head, and stopped her thinking about other things.

Mr Gupta was expecting her at noon. At five to, Polly crawled under her desk. It was as safe a place as any. She sat curled in a ball, her head on her knees, and waited for the day to inch away from her, to join all the other days she could barely remember. Sitting under her desk was weird. She knew that. But nothing in her life was rational right now. It was just dark. The light at the top of her well shaft seemed to be dimming, like she was falling further and deeper with every passing minute.

Her phone buzzed insistently at ten past, then again at half past. Polly stayed where she was, ignoring the sound. Her legs were growing tired. She needed to stretch them. She crawled from under the desk and lay full length on the floor instead, playing with the tufts of carpet beneath her fingers.

Everyone would be better off without me.

Her phone was blinking from its position by her bed. Polly tapped the screen and stared at the string of messages. Four missed calls from Ollie. Three texts from Mr Gupta.

You're late.
Mr Gupta.

Where are you? The wedding has begun.
Mr Gupta.

Polly, get in touch as soon as possible.
Mr Gupta.

Polly crawled into bed and wrapped herself up tightly in her duvet.

Everyone would be better off without me.

She must have slept for a while. When she woke

up, Ollie was talking to her. At least, she could hear his voice. She propped herself up blearily and gazed around. She *could* hear Ollie, but he wasn't in the room with her. He was outside her room.

". . .let her sleep a little while longer, Ollie."

"That's all she's doing. Sleeping. Something's not right."

"We're worried about her too, love. But sleep is a good healer. You should go home now."

"I'm staying." Ollie sounded stubborn. "She'll come out of her room eventually. She'll talk to me then, I know she will."

The conversation grew more indistinct. Her mother was going downstairs, but Ollie was still outside the door. She could feel him.

Polly swung her legs off the bed and shuffled across her room, hugging her duvet tightly around herself. She wanted to hear his voice, but she didn't want him to see her. So she contented herself with cracking open her bedroom door and peeping through.

A little way down the corridor, Ollie was sitting on the landing with his hand in his blond hair. He was on the phone.

"Tomorrow. Ten o'clock. I've needed you so badly this week, Lila, thank God you're coming home... You picked the worst time to go on holiday... No, don't talk to her. She mustn't know. It will be too much for her, I think."

Polly felt the blood draining from her face. Ollie was waiting for Polly to come out of her room so he could tell her it was over.

Her boyfriend still loved Lila. Polly could hear it in the heartfelt tone in his voice as he told Lila over and over how much he'd missed her, how much he needed her... He had always loved Lila. Ollie and Lila, Lila and Ollie. The golden couple, back together the way things were supposed to be. The way things could be again. Planning their secret date at the beach. They would kiss. They would forget Polly had ever existed.

EIGHTEEN

Polly had never known such a long night. She lay, awake and watchful, as the clock ticked through the hours. She listened to the sound of traffic as it slowed and trickled and disappeared altogether. When there was no traffic left to listen to, she could hear the sea, a faint but insistent murmur through the night.

I should be feeling something, she thought. *My boyfriend is leaving me. He's getting back together with my best friend.*

But she didn't have any tears left to cry. So she lay, and watched, and thought about what she was going to do, and waited for the birds to herald the morning.

"You're up!" her mother exclaimed as Polly walked

into the kitchen, her freshly showered hair dripping on her shoulders. "And showered!"

"Did I smell so bad?" Polly asked a little drily as she helped herself to an orange from the chiller drawer in the fridge.

She could see her mother trying to backtrack. "Of course not, love . . . It's just . . . I'm glad to see you."

Polly concentrated on peeling her orange. She needed to peel the whole thing in one long curly strip. If she broke the strip, something bad might happen. "Like you said," she replied as her fingers carefully pulled the peel from the fruit, "I had to get up some time."

"What are your plans today?"

Polly's nail slipped. She regarded the half-strip of peel that lay on the table in front of her. "I thought I might go to the beach," she said.

"Great idea. Why don't you call your friends and see if they'll meet you there?"

Stop trying so hard, Mum. "Nine's a bit early for my friends."

Lila would be blow-drying her hair and putting on a cute little summer dress and applying her make-up, she reflected. It always took Lila at least an hour to get ready for any important event in her life. Ollie would dash out of the house at five to ten without even brushing his hair. But with his warm smile and his deep blue eyes, he would be perfect as he was. They would run into each other's arms in the secret cove.

Polly mustn't know. . .

She has to know some time. . .

"So you're going there by yourself?"

Polly shrugged. "I could use the fresh air."

Beth and her mother hovered in the hallway as Polly collected her bag and keys.

"See you later then," said Polly's mum.

Now that she had decided to go the beach, Polly wanted to get there as soon as possible. The beach felt like a destination. When she got there, she would wait and she would see Ollie and Lila together and she would let them know that it was OK. She wanted them to be happy.

There were a few people walking on the beach when Polly got there, exercising their dogs or taking a stroll, flying kites and building sandcastles. Getting on with their lives. Polly made her way past the town clock. Although she hadn't heard Ollie specify the secret cove, she knew that's where he and Lila would go. It was romantic, and private. It was perfect.

The crowds, such as they were, thinned away to nothing as Polly made her way along the path to the cove. The sun was warm already, beating down on her head. The sea shone like burnished metal as the tide washed calmly along the shore.

No one was here. It was gone ten o'clock. Perhaps Ollie and Lila had met already. Perhaps even now they were walking hand in hand up the cliff path, away from the sea and back to the town. She was too late.

Setting her shoes on a rock, her bag and jacket beside them, Polly walked down to the edge of the water. The sand was cool between her bare toes. The water felt soft and inviting around her ankles.

Somewhere out there is America, she thought, gazing at the horizon. *Is Dad on the beach, looking out to sea too?* And then she remembered that in California it was two o'clock in the morning.

The sea had always calmed Polly. Watching the waves was like a meditation. All her problems seemed to fade away when she watched the surf rise and crash and rise again, endless and patient and perfect.

It would keep rising and falling, over and over again. There was comfort in that. No matter what she did, the waves would keep rising and falling until the end of the world.

Polly started wading. She was in a dress, but it didn't seem to matter. The water was cold as it crept up her legs, her thighs, up to her belly. She reached out her hands and dived into the waves, feeling the pull of the surf on the fabric of her dress. It was strange, swimming in her clothes. Reckless, but nice. As she turned over on her back and floated in the water, feeling her hair fan out around her head and tasting the salt on her lips, she felt as if she could just fall asleep as she was, her arms and legs spread out like a starfish, her dress swirling like seaweed around her limbs. Polly felt peaceful and detached. She could feel the current moving her further out from the shore. She would twist and eddy like driftwood on the sea's moving surface, leaving her mess of a life behind on the shore. One day, she might even wash up in California.

You can't float away from your problems. Your problems are inside yourself. Wherever you go, you take your problems with you.

"Everyone would be better off without me," Polly told the sky.

She let herself sink.

The bright light dimmed as her head went beneath the waves. The light was still bright, but with a blue tinge that was growing darker, the deeper she went. And then. . .

Her lungs were burning. Screaming for air. Her arms and legs began to beat at the water. Opening her eyes, Polly stared in sudden shock at the rippling blue world around her. The undercurrents were pushing and pulling at her.

The air was up. She needed to go up. But which way was up?

NINETEEN

Panic took hold. Polly would have screamed, but if she opened her mouth the sea would rush in. Her lungs would pump and suck in desperation, hoping for air but finding only salt and water and cold blue death. She would drown. She would float, lifeless, back to the surface, for her screaming friends to find. Like Ryan not so many months ago: hair like seaweed and eyes closed in a chalk-white face. Dead. Gone. For ever.

Isn't that what you want? said the silky voice in her head. *For all the pain to go away?*

And in that moment, Polly knew the answer was no. Life surged through her, insistent and determined. But where was the air? Where was the surface? Everything was blue. And everything was so cold. . .

Her locket swung heavy against her collarbone. She reaching up to touch its carved surface as the water tumbled around her. The necklace was wet and cold, hard and real, and as she touched it, Ollie's face swam before her through the washing light. His eyes were the same colour as the waves that were pulling her away from him. Her mother was there too, and Beth, and her father. . . All her friends. . . Lila's explosive giggles, Eve's auburn sheen of hair. . . She could even hear the strains of Rhi's guitar, pure and lovely above the restless sea. Everyone she loved. Everyone she was leaving.

Polly reached for them all, but they vanished in the ripples. Her vision was closing around her as her body fought to breathe. How ironic that now, more than at any time in her life, she wanted to live.

With one last desperate lunge, she burst to the surface, coughing and choking. Where was the shore? All she could see was water. Her dress was heavy, dragging her downwards. She had to resist. She had to find the strength from somewhere. . .

A line of cliffs and rocks on the horizon. *Not far*, Polly told herself, trying to coordinate her heavy limbs. *Not far at all.*

How could she have let things get this bad? What had she thought she was doing? She of all people knew what the death of a friend did to the ones left behind. Hadn't she seen for herself Lila's devastation and guilt? Josh's pinched and haunted face as he had held Ryan's lifeless body in his arms? How could she be so selfish as to wish that on anyone?

And Ollie. Poor Ollie. Loving Ollie had been one of the best things that had ever happened to her. If he wanted Lila, she would have to cope with that because she loved him and she wanted him to be happy. . .

The shore didn't feel as if it was getting any closer, no matter how hard she tried to swim. The current didn't want to return to shore. The tide had turned. The sea had other places to go.

Not far, Polly repeated to herself mechanically as the current pulled her back time and time again. No matter how hard she swam, the shoreline was receding. She really was tired now. It was all she could do to keep her head above the water. In a single moment of horrible clarity, she realized that she didn't have the strength to make it to shore.

A voice was calling her across the waves.

"POLLY! Polly, hold on, I'm coming . . . I'M COMING!"

Polly was starting to feel sleepy. Ollie's voice was just a dream, she knew. It was such a lovely voice, so deep and full. She could listen to it for ever.

"POLLY!"

The water washed over her face, making her choke. This would all be so easy if she just stopped fighting. . . *Lovely dream*, she thought wistfully, as her body sank lower and lower in the waves. *Lovely Ollie*.

A slick blond head was coming towards her through the sea, strong arms cleaving the water. Ollie was swimming towards her, shouting her name.

I'm hallucinating as well as hearing things, Polly thought dimly.

But she found herself opening her mouth, trying to call for him and getting a mouthful of seawater for her troubles. She choked and spat and tried to keep breathing. She wanted to wave at Ollie but her arms were too tired to hold up out of the water. This was too difficult. Her body was so cold now she was losing all sensation in her legs. Her dress felt like lead. The sea was so insistent, so beguiling, curling around her and tugging her down into its depths.

Just let yourself sink. Like you did the first time. . .

The sea washed over her face again, more strongly this time. She stopped moving her arms and began to sink below the surface. She didn't want to, but she couldn't help it.

A strong arm came around her and hauled her upwards.

"Got you . . . I've got you . . . Hold on to me, Polly, you're safe now. . ."

Polly choked and cried as the seawater stung the back of her nose and throat. "Ollie," she croaked, holding on to him with cold, sluggish fingers. "You're real. . ."

"Shh, just concentrate on staying afloat with me, Poll . . . Plenty of time to talk when we get to shore. Lie back now . . . Trust me. . ."

Polly lay back, her arms and legs completely spent, and let Ollie pull her through the water. The sky above was beautiful, calm and blue, and she watched it until her shoulders bumped against the coarse sand and her legs trailed in the surf and she could roll on to her stomach to cough and retch up half the ocean.

Beside her Ollie was coughing too, his breath coming in shallow ragged gasps. Polly tried to get on to her feet, but settled for crawling on her hands and knees up the beach to drier sand, her hair hanging heavy and cold around her face and her locket swinging. Then somehow she was upright, and Ollie was too, his chilled arms around her holding her close as he murmured her name against her hair, and her cheeks, and her lips.

"Polly, my love, Polly, Polly, Polly, Lila saw you in the sea, thank God we were there. . ."

His lips were as cold as ice but his mouth was like fire. Polly kissed him back with every part of what little strength she had left. They fitted together like two halves of one whole, his arms big and strong around her back and his wet hair thick and shining between her fingers. Their kiss tasted of love and intense relief, but of sadness too.

And then the world dimmed again and everything went black.

TWENTY

The air smelled strange, the sheets felt scratchy against her skin. Polly opened her eyes and gazed at the strip light on the pale green ceiling. Her throat felt rough and her head rougher. She wasn't dead, she assumed. You didn't feel rough when you were dead, presumably. Which probably meant that she was alive.

I never meant for it to get this far. Memories of the sea flooded her, and she recoiled from them in shame and fear and relief, and flung her hands up to cover her eyes.

"Where am I?" she whispered against her palms.

"You're in the hospital, Polly."

Polly lowered her hands from her dry, salt-reddened

eyes, and stared at Lila's mum sitting on a chair beside her bed. There was no one else in the room.

"Why are you here?" she asked. Her question probably sounded a little rude. She knew the answer; Lila's mum was here in her therapist role. She just wasn't sure if she was willing to acknowledge that.

Lila's mum smiled. "Waiting for you to wake up. There are a lot of people who will be very pleased to hear that you're back with us again. They're in the waiting room right now."

Polly rubbed her eyes. "What people?"

"Your mother for one. Beth. All your friends. Ollie, of course." Lila's mother cocked her head and studied Polly with gentle eyes. "Your dad is on a flight as we speak. He should be here in the morning."

Polly sank back into her pillows and stared at the strip light. The thought of all those people waiting to see her was troubling. Her father was coming all the way from America. How could she look any of them in the eye after what she had so nearly done?

"I thought seeing everyone at once would be too overwhelming for you," Lila's mother said, accurately reading Polly's uncertain expression. "They will be there until you feel ready to see them. There is no rush, Polly. You can do this in your own time."

"I bet you had trouble persuading Mum to stay in the waiting room," Polly whispered.

Lila's mother laughed. "You could say that. But she could see the sense of not overwhelming you to begin with."

Polly remembered her mother bandaging her knee when she fell on their apartment steps in San Francisco. The bright red blood had seemed so horrifying to her at the age of seven, but her mother had cuddled her and mopped the blood away and soon they had been eating a biscuit and her leg had stopped aching. Tears blurred her eyes at the memory.

"Do you want to talk about anything, Polly?" Lila's mother asked.

When Polly opened her mouth this time, everything came pouring out at once. Her dad and Courtney, Willow and Ollie, her memories of San Francisco and her confused feelings, how she couldn't control her emotions, her panic attack on Alcatraz. That terrible day at the farm when she couldn't breathe, and the shock of returning home to find Beth had moved in. The new colour of the kitchen, the smell of paint in the air, the feeling that it wasn't her home any more. The feeling that everything was changing. The feeling that she wasn't enough, she'd never be good enough, she'd never belong. She always felt there was something wrong about her, that things that were so easy for other people made her so anxious. She was tired of feeling anxious about everything. She wanted to talk about her fears over Ollie and Lila too, but she remembered who she was talking to just in time. That would have to wait for another day.

Lila's mother simply sat quietly and said nothing as Polly talked and talked. And that was fine, because Polly knew she was listening. That was all that seemed to matter.

"I have been so lost," Polly said at last, feeling completely drained after what felt like hours of spilling her soul. "Like I've been somewhere far away, and no one could see me or hear me."

"I'm hearing you."

It was the first thing Lila's mother had said since Polly had started talking. And Polly felt such relief that she wanted to cry. A sort of calm spread through her as she rested her head back on her pillow and let her tears flow down her face. All her fears were out there now, in the form of words that had been both spoken and heard. And somehow they didn't seem so scary any more, or so unbearable. She'd always thought that asking for help proved that you were weak, that you couldn't cope by yourself. She could see how wrong-headed that was now. She felt a relief she hadn't had in a long time, and it made her stronger somehow.

"Thank you," she said. The phrase didn't begin to cover it, but it the best that she had.

"Any time." Lila's mother took Polly's hand and squeezed it. "How do you feel now, Polly?"

"Tired," Polly said, squeezing back gratefully. "But a little better. Talking to you has really helped."

"I can see that. There's someone that I'd like you to meet, Polly. Someone you can talk to like this, on a more regular basis. Would you do that?"

"You mean, like a therapist?" Polly asked, blushing a little.

Lila's mother nodded. "It shouldn't be me because you already know me too well."

"And I would just . . . talk to them?" Polly checked.

"Like I talked to you?" It couldn't be that easy, could it?

"Absolutely. A good therapist will make sure you feel completely safe saying what you need to say," said Lila's mother, standing up. "I'll be in touch with a list for you, Polly. You should find someone that you feel comfortable with. It might take a few meetings, but you'll get there. Now, is there anything I can get you before I go?"

There was, Polly realized.

"Can you get Ollie?" she asked shyly.

She was too tired to get out of bed to check her reflection, or brush her teeth, or do any of the hundred things people usually did whenever they were about to see their boyfriends. Was Ollie even her boyfriend any more? She wanted to thank him, regardless. He had saved her life and she would never forget that.

When he came in, Ollie seemed too big for the room. He was too tanned, too healthy-looking to be in a hospital, even as a visitor. His eyes were troubled.

"Hi," he said after a moment.

Polly wanted so badly to kiss him, to put her arms

around him and apologise for putting him through so much. "Hi," was all she managed to say back.

He perched a little gingerly on the chair beside her bed, his hands in his lap. There was an awkward silence. Polly wondered where to start.

"Thank you for saving my life," she said at last, smiling tentatively at him.

Ollie fiddled with his ear. "No problem."

"It *was* a problem," Polly corrected. "But it's not a problem any more. I'm going to work really hard at getting better, Ollie. You deserve that from me. I deserve it."

"I'm glad," he said. But he looked sad as he said it.

Polly steeled herself. "If you want to break up with me, I'll understand. You and Lila are probably a better combination than you and me anyway."

Ollie rubbed his eyes. "Why do we keep having this conversation?" he asked, looking directly at her now. "I'm not interested in Lila."

"But you were meeting her—"

"I was meeting her to talk about *you*," he said. "I was worried about *you*."

Polly felt a little surge of hope. Maybe their sad

little kiss at the beach hadn't been a goodbye kiss after all.

"I am so *mad* at you for scaring me like that," he suddenly burst out, making Polly jump a little. "Why didn't you talk to me? Why didn't you tell me more about how you were feeling? What would I have done if I'd lost you? What then?"

Polly saw with some wonder that there were tears in his eyes. Ollie was crying. Over her.

"I . . . I don't know," she stammered, feeling awful.

Ollie wiped his eyes fiercely. "I still love you, Poll," he said. "But I'm not sure I'm the best thing for you right now. I don't know how to help you and it seems like whatever I do makes it worse. I think you might need to help yourself first, you know?"

Of course she knew. How could she not?

"I'm so sorry," she whispered, as her heart broke inside her. "About everything. Truly, I am."

TWENTY-ONE

It was a good thing that she didn't suffer from hayfever, Polly reflected, lying in her own bed at home. There were so many flowers in the room, she would have been sneezing her head off. She loved the flowers, but she felt bad too, every time she looked at their bright colours and happy, nodding heads.

"Stop feeling guilty," said Lila, looking up from painting her nails as she sprawled across the end of Polly's bed. "People *like* giving flowers or they wouldn't do it."

"How do you know that's what I was thinking?" Polly asked, startled.

"Because I can read minds," said Lila in a spooky

161

voice. She made a witchy claw with her hands lifted into the air, the polish wet and gleaming.

Sitting on the floor with their backs to the furniture, Rhi and Eve exchanged glances.

"Read mine then, Madame Murray," Eve suggested.

Lila furrowed her brow and stared hard at Eve. "You are thinking right now that I'm a total idiot."

"It's a miracle, you're one hundred per cent right," Eve grinned, making both Lila and Rhi laugh.

Polly smiled a little awkwardly. It was great to see her friends, but weird too. It was hard to know what they were thinking. *They must think I'm crazy*, she thought.

"Even I can read your mind right now, Polly," Eve said, rousing Polly from her thoughts. "You're wondering why we're still friends with someone who's even more of an idiot than Lila."

"Don't call Polly an idiot," said Rhi, looking a little worried.

Eve being her usual blunt and caustic self made Polly feel much better than if Eve had tiptoed around her in a completely un-Eve-ish way. She laughed with real amusement. "I am an idiot," she confessed. "I freely admit it."

"Excellent," said Eve in approval. "In that case, I'm still your friend."

"Your mum was so great in the hospital," Polly said, turning to Lila. "I know I've still got about a million problems, but as long as I talk about them I think I'm going to be all right."

"Mum's always trying her listening face on me," Lila said, rolling her eyes. "I don't think it works when you're related." She looked more serious. "But I'm really glad it worked for you, Poll."

Eve and Rhi both joined Lila on Polly's bed. Rhi took Polly's hand and squeezed it tightly. They all smiled at each other, and Polly felt warm and loved and safe.

"It must have been so awful," Rhi said sympathetically. "I'm so sorry we weren't there for you when you needed us."

"I needed to recognize my problem first," Polly said, smiling at Rhi.

"When did you first start feeling so bad, Polly?" Lila asked.

Polly considered the question. It was an interesting one. "Probably when Mum and Dad first split up," she admitted, thinking back. "I felt abandoned. I thought I'd dealt with those feelings, but they all came back when I went to California. The rest of it just kind of followed. I still need to talk it through about a hundred more times, and work it out. I had my first appointment with one of the therapists your mum recommended this morning, Lila. She was really great."

It had been wonderful, talking everything through again. Just like Lila's mother, the new therapist had listened and gently probed, and once again Polly had felt freer and happier for having got the words out into the world for someone to hear.

"Why didn't you talk to us about it?" For once, Eve's question was gentle.

"A lot of it kicked off when I went away," Polly told her friends. "And you were all busy when I got back."

"What's been the worst feeling?" asked Rhi.

The answer to that one was easy. "The anxiety. It felt like this great weight, pressing down on me. Sometimes, I couldn't breathe."

"I felt like that when Dad was arrested," said Eve. She studied her perfectly manicured nails. "Those first few days . . . I'd never had a situation so completely out of my control before. It was awful." She looked at Rhi. "How did you cope when your sister died?"

"The pain of Ruth's death never goes away," Rhi admitted, "but some days I cope with it better than others. It's easier when I talk about her, I think."

"Like now?" Polly asked, and Rhi nodded.

"I used to think I could cope with anything," Lila said, rolling back on Polly's bed. "That I was invincible, somehow. Then there was all that awful business when we had to leave London, and the shock of moving to Heartside, and Ryan's death. . ."

Everyone fell silent, remembering Ryan. And Polly looked at her friends and felt warm and supported all over again. Everyone had problems, and everyone had to find ways to deal with them. That was life. As strange as it seemed, acknowledging her worries made her feel so much better than trying to supress them.

There was a quiet knock at the door.

"I think Polly needs some rest now, girls," said Polly's mother.

There was a brief flurry of hugs and squeezed hands as Eve, Rhi and Lila all left with promises to call

Polly later. It was Polly's dad who saw them all to the front door, while her mum fussed around her bed and straightened her pillows.

Polly hadn't quite got her head around the fact that her parents were in the same house again. The last time her dad had visited England, there had been the most awful fights. But since her mother had started seeing Beth, she had seemed happier and more inclined to smile whenever Polly's father was mentioned. Seeing them together now – working together for Polly's benefit – felt odd, but nice.

"Your dad and I wondered if we could talk to you, Polly love," said her mother as her dad reappeared in the bedroom to lean against the door frame.

"We're both so sorry," her dad put in. He glanced at Polly's mum, as if looking for reassurance. "We were both so busy creating our new lives that we didn't see what was happening to you."

"We feel terrible," said Polly's mother, sitting down on the bed. "Beth told me off earlier for not including you in our plans for her to move in. I thought it would be a nice surprise. . ." She tailed off, biting her lip.

"It *was* a nice surprise," Polly reassured her. "But

when I came back, I was just pretty jet-lagged, and confused, and everything was just a bit too much. I do really like Beth, Mum – you know I do. It's so great to see how happy you are together."

Her mother looked relieved.

"What about me and Courtney?" asked her dad.

Polly knew that her parents had had a long conversation almost as soon as her dad had made it through the door from his early morning flight. Her mother knew about Courtney and Willow now.

"That was harder," Polly said honestly. "But if Courtney makes you happy, Dad, then I'm happy too."

She looked at her parents, both gazing so anxiously at her with such love and guilt in their eyes. She belonged to these two people, whoever they were with and wherever they lived. She knew that now.

"Promise to tell us if you ever feel this low again," said her mother.

"Promise us," her dad echoed.

"I promise," Polly said. "But truly. I'm going to be fine." And she really meant it.

TWENTY-TWO

Polly spent the rest of Tuesday taking it easy. There was no point in rushing anything. She made some new clothes to replace the designs her dad had been selling in the States, and painted some hangers. She sketched too, new designs full of Californian inspiration: sea birds and sun umbrellas, redwood trees and fruit. It was peaceful, just drawing and sewing. By letting her mind dwell only on which part to sew next, and which button to place where, Polly could feel herself starting to heal.

She woke up on Wednesday morning to the sound of a text. Yawning, she fumbled on her bedside table for her phone.

Beach at 10 this morning?

O x

Polly sat up, wide awake. She hadn't heard a word from Ollie since their conversation at the hospital on Monday, when he told her that he needed some time by himself. And now he was texting, and inviting her to the beach. She tried to squash the excitement bubbling in her chest. She couldn't get ahead of herself. This might be a new start, but it might be an end instead. She didn't want to think about that, but forced herself to face reality. If it wasn't a date . . . perhaps Ollie was going to break up with her for good.

She closed her eyes and focused on stilling the anxiety that was starting to swirl around in the pit of her belly. What would be, would be. She couldn't control Ollie's feelings. Whatever he decided, she would respect that. And she was strong enough to survive.

It was eight-thirty, and the sun was already climbing the blue August sky as Polly hurried into the shower. She conditioned her hair carefully, and applied a touch of make-up. Considering her wardrobe, she resisted the temptation to put on an outfit that she knew Ollie loved: a strapless dress with a sweetheart neckline covered in sprigged red flowers. She couldn't jinx this by trying to please someone else. It was too important. So she chose something that *she* liked instead: a cotton dress the colour of the bluest California sky. Slipping her feet into her favourite sandals, she dried her hair so that it lay smoothly on her head and fixed it with a pale pink hairclip she had picked up at the market. A touch of eyeliner, some mascara, and she was as ready as she would ever be.

Polly studied herself in the mirror. A pale face with wide hazel eyes, smooth blonde hair, a pink hairclip and a freckled nose gazed back.

This is me, she thought. *Flaws and all.*

She grabbed something to eat to settle her stomach, which was fluttering with nerves. Then she picked up her bag and her keys and let herself out of the house.

She hadn't been outside much since her trip to hospital. It was uncomfortable, thinking about the last time she had walked down the street and through the town towards the beach. Her mind then had been dark, and nearly empty of feeling. Catching sight of her pale face in a shop window as she made her way along Marine Parade towards the clock tower, Polly straightened her shoulders and reminded herself: that was then. This was now.

When she saw the opening to the path that led to the cove, Polly realized her legs were feeling wobbly and her breath was starting to come in shallow gasps. She sat down for a moment at the foot of the clock tower and closed her eyes. Her therapist had told her that whenever she felt anxious, she had to find a place in her mind where she felt safe.

Ollie, she thought silently. Whether he was hers or not, he could always be her safe place. The love and care that he had shown for her would always warm her heart and calm her thoughts, whether they were together or apart. Just touching the locket that she still wore around her neck was enough to bring her back from the edge.

He had given her so much. She had given him so little in return.

Determined to face whatever lay ahead, Polly resumed her walk. Down on to the beach and along the path towards the secret cove. Gulls squabbling on the shore flew away as she rounded the corner on to the golden rock-strewn sands and stood for a moment, catching her breath.

Ollie's familiar silhouette was standing by the water's edge. He looked lonely, gazing out across the sparkling waves that lapped at his feet.

He's thinking of me, Polly realized. She felt so overcome with love for him that her rising tears threatened to choke her.

It felt like a long walk down the smooth sand. Ollie turned as she approached, sensing that she was there with no need for words. Polly soaked him in as they gazed at each other, wordless and intense. The aqua of his eyes and his deeply tanned skin and the way his hair stood in whipped blond peaks around his lovely, familiar face.

I trust this boy. I love him.

It seemed so clear to Polly now just what she had almost thrown away. She wanted to throw herself down in the sand and beat her hands against the ground for how stupid she had been. But she couldn't change the past. She could just try to make a better future.

Ollie moved swiftly towards her. Polly's heart lurched with happiness at the look in his eyes. She saw the love there as his arms came around her. His hands gently stroked her hair, and his mouth dipped towards hers. Polly felt dizzy with emotion as he kissed her, lifting her off the sand, holding her so tight she wondered if he ever planned on letting go.

Hope raged through Polly like a summer storm as she kissed him back. *Please don't let this be goodbye,* she thought.

"Hello you," he whispered, after pressing one last kiss to her mouth. He sounded breathless.

"I love you," Polly tumbled out before she lost her nerve. "Ollie, I love you so much. I'll never forget you, or the time we've had together. But I know that you might need more than I can give right now and—"

He silenced her with another kiss even more passionate than before. Polly lost her powers of speech completely as she clung to him, feeling the weight of him and the strength of him.

"I've said it before and I'll say it again," he said when he pulled back to take a breath. "When are we going to stop having this conversation? I love you more than anything, Polly. I always have and I always will. I'll still be telling you this next week, next month, next year. If you don't want to be with me, that's a different matter. But if you think I deserve someone else, you couldn't be more wrong."

"But how can you put up with me?" she half-laughed, half-sobbed, clinging to the hope that this was real and he was still here with his arms around her and his eyes blazing blue fire. "I must drive you mad!"

"Believe me," said Ollie with feeling, "you do. But in a good way."

He kissed her again, and the sweetness and intensity of it gave Polly the shivers.

"Nothing you can do or say will drive me away," he said between kisses. "We're meant to be together. So you'd better start believing it or I'll have to throw you back in the sea where I found you on Sunday."

He scooped her up, taking her whole weight in his arms as easily as if she were a feather, and started running towards the water.

"No!" Polly squealed, her whole body coursing with delight and terror, "don't do it, don't throw me in, this is my favourite outfit. . ."

Ollie was still running, showering kisses on Polly's head as she kicked pointlessly against him. "Promise you'll stop trying to dump me or I'll dump *you*. In the water."

She was able to nod. Without qualifications, without anxiety. Polly gloried in the peace and the magic of this feeling of certainty. She could do this on her own. But with Ollie by her side, it would be even better. They would fight her demons and send them running. She was strong and smart, and as lucky as she was to have Ollie, he was lucky to have her too. She didn't want to forget that. She wouldn't.

"I promise!" she gasped, hiccupping with tears and laughter at the same time. "I promise I'll stop trying to dump you! I'll never dump you again!"

Ollie stopped at the very edge of the water and kissed her soundly one more time. The kiss was full and deep and, finally, satisfied. It was the purest, sweetest kiss Polly had ever known.

"It's about time we got that straight," he said.

LOOK OUT FOR MORE

HEARTSIDE BAY

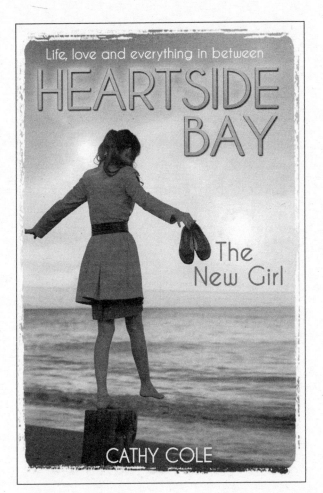

Life, love and everything in between

HEARTSIDE BAY

The New Girl

CATHY COLE

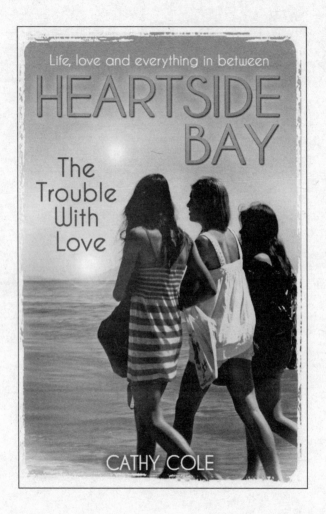

Life, love and everything in between

HEARTSIDE BAY

The
Trouble
With
Love

CATHY COLE

Life, love and everything in between

HEARTSIDE BAY

More
Than a
Love
Song

CATHY COLE

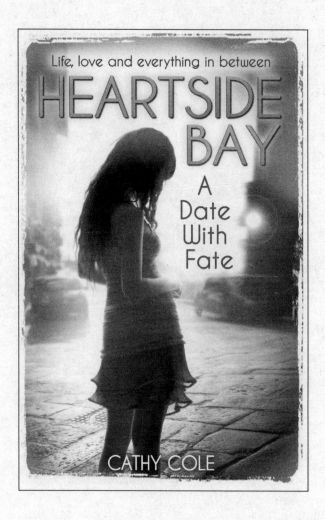

Life, love and everything in between

HEARTSIDE BAY

A Date With Fate

CATHY COLE

Life, love and everything in between

HEARTSIDE BAY

Never
a Perfect
Moment

CATHY COLE

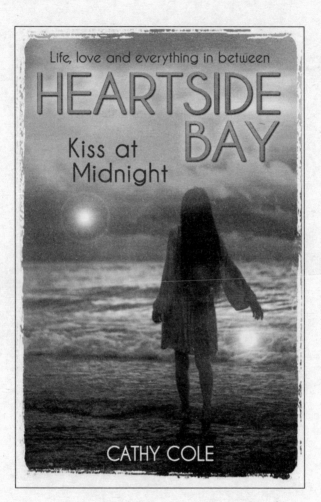

Life, love and everything in between

HEARTSIDE BAY

Kiss at Midnight

CATHY COLE

Life, love and everything in between

HEARTSIDE BAY

Back to You

CATHY COLE

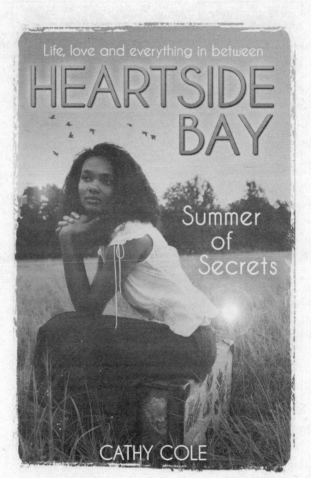

Life, love and everything in between

HEARTSIDE BAY

Summer of Secrets

CATHY COLE

Life, love and everything in between

HEARTSIDE BAY

Playing the Game

CATHY COLE